HOOKS
AND
BULLETS
AND
DYING EMBERS

by
JACK KERINS

Illustrated By
Pete Johnson

Copyright © 2005 Jack Kerins

Published by
BRIARWOOD PUBLICATIONS
82 Briarwood
Terre Haute, IN 47803

Library of Congress Cataloging-in-Publication

"Hooks and Bullets and Dying Embers"
Illustrations by Pete Johnson
Cover Photos by Jack Kerins

FIRST EDITION

ISBN 0-9633962-4-2
Printed in the United States of America by
United Graphics Incorporated
P.O. Box 559
Mattoon, IL 61938

TO

ELYNORE PETYO KERINS

1928 – 2003

… my "Pet", for fifty-three years, put up with my wanderings, listened to my ravings, comforted my moanings, and proofread my writings. All, often with comments, but seldom with complaints.

I loved that girl dearly, and I always will.

ACKNOWLEDGEMENT

A special thank you to my daughter
Kathy Kerins Neal,
without whose help and encouragement
this book would never have come to be.

PART I
OF FISH AND FISHERMEN

PART II
OF HUNTS AND HUNTERS

PART III
OF PONDERING AND PORTAGING

AUTHOR'S NOTE

I have been a member of the OUTDOOR WRITERS ASSOCIATION OF AMERICA since 1966, but did not attend a conference until 1975. I made it to the next seventeen before I missed another.

However, it was at breakfast on the morning of that first meeting that I listened to my good friend, Homer Circle, recite the OWAA PRAYER.

I was so impressed by those words, I have murmured them every morning since.

So it is here, with the permission of the author, Margaret Menamin, and the members of the OWAA Board of Directors, I wish to share them with you here on the opposite page

OWAA PRAYER

(Outdoor Writers Association of America)

by

Margaret Menamin

God, give me stillness, give me time to stand
Unpressed by creed and credits, and undefiled
By dust of industry, and be a child,
Reminded of my oneness with the land.
Let me put forth fresh blossoms from my hand.
Let me lose not my kinship with the wild.

And if I should call this mine, remind me, God,
That it is only that my blood and bone are mine,
Not mine to waste, not mine to own,
But simply mine to be. I am the goldenrod, the
    grain, the granite. I am stream and glen.
Remind me to preserve myself. Amen.

INTRODUCTION

Those of us old enough to remember the years prior to the Great Depression have witnessed the most exciting and rapidly changing eras in all of history.

Life was simple during our boyhood days in the rural Midwest. Possessions were few, and dreams of personal adventure were boundless. Legendary tales of the colorful characters and events that dominated the latter half of the 19th century were still very much in the forefront. Factual or fictitious, stories of Civil War battles, Custer's stand at the Little Big Horn and dramatic accounts of frontier life weighed heavily on young emotions and imaginations.

Before we realized it, our adolescent years were behind us. As young adults, we added our own pages to history by participating in the greatest global conflict of all times. It culminated with our sudden introduction to the atomic age.

In a single life span, we had seen everything from the use of coal oil lamps and travel by horseback to that of neon lighted cities and space vehicles carrying men to the moon. It is almost difficult to comprehend, but it's all true, and damned if we weren't there to actually witness it all!

The following stories are mostly of my peacetime adventures in the great outdoors. Certain descriptions may have been enhanced a tad here and there for dramatic effect, but for the most, they are all true. The names of some individuals have been changed in an attempt to protect the personal integrity of those who need it most – bless 'em all.

**PART I
OF FISH AND FISHERMEN**

"The hours a man spends while fishing are not deducted from those of his lifespan."

Author Unknown

HEARING THE CALL

Along about green-up each year, when the spring wild flowers first open tiny faces to a warming sun and there is a freshness in the air following a lingering winter, it comes to me. At first it's hardly more than a sensation, but it's there just the same.

The longer I ignore it, the more persistent and imploring it becomes. Its muted pleas seem to be echoed over and over again until I drop whatever it is I'm doing, pick up my tackle, and cut out for the nearest lake. For what I hear is a fish softly calling my name.

"You've got to be some kind of a nut," says Pet. "You never seem to hear anything I tell you when there's something to be done around here, and

3

you're certainly not hearing anything now. Besides, fish can't talk."

Perhaps she's right, about my mental status that is, but to me; the call can never be more vividly clear. It comes to me on the balmy, southwest breezes of April and I hear it in the music of birdsong emanating from the fresh, green branches of the hardwoods. It resonates from the unfolding blossoms of the redbuds and dogwoods and from the trickling run-off of winter's melt and gentle spring showers.

"It's impossible to hear such a thing," Pet insists. "Believe me I know! It's simply one of your lame-brained excuses for getting out of work."

There is a ring of authority in her voice, for she is a retired speech and hearing pathologist. If a sound cannot be measured in decibels on her audiometer, as far as she is concerned, it just plain isn't there for the human ear to hear.

"How can you be sure?" I argue. "Haven't you ever read about the theory of sensory perception?

"You know the one that asks if there is such a thing as sound when no one is around to hear it? Like when a tree falls in a forest, is there really a noise if there is no ear present to pick up the vibrations?

"Maybe it works something like that - only in reverse, kinda. Maybe, somehow I've been gifted to hear sounds

4

you and that thing-a-me-bob gadget of yours don't. Maybe..."

"If I remember correctly," Pet interrupts, "that same stupid theory also questions the tree's very existence if there is no eye there to see it."

"And, if it's MAYBES you want," she continues, "maybe you get these kookier, harebrained ideas from banging your head against too many trees that aren't supposed to be there."

"Surely the world's great philosophers were all unmarried," I mumble to myself as Pet stomps out of the room.

If there is no such thing as a fish's call, why then would a young boy risk the punishment for playing hooky from school so he can spend a spring day with a cane pole and bobber on a farm pond in Iowa?

And, why would a man, dressed in a business suit, doff is coat, roll up his sleeves, and take a rod and reel from the trunk of his car to cast from the concrete walks along the Boardman River in the heart of Traverse City, Michigan?

Why, too, would a bib overalled farmer skip a precious day of spring planting to spend it in a johnboat on a strip pit in southern Indiana?

The call of a fish is not just limited to spring, either. It is fickle and wandering plea. I have heard it at various times and in unpredictable places.

HEARING THE CALL

It has come to me while standing in a sporting goods store feeling the action of a classic split cane fly rod. And, I've heard it when patching my hip boots and while thumbing through the pages of a road atlas. I've heard it in the crackling flames of burning logs and in the classic writings of McClane, and Schwiebert, and Haig-Brown. Occasionally, I have even heard the call faintly emanating from the clear pool of an idle martini.

The call has come to me from near and far and from various species of fish. From bass, bluegill, and crappie in the farm ponds near my home. And, I have heard speckled trout and arctic char calling to me from the Kogaluk River in northern Quebec.

Invitations have come to me from tarpon and snook in the rivers and lagoons of Costa Rica and from giant lake trout in the waters of Great Bear in the Northwest Territories. And big rainbows and browns have begged me to return once again to Tongariro in New Zealand.

All I know is, for those of us who hear them, the calls of the fishes are real, and when we hear them, we must somehow respond.

It's little wonder Pet shakes her head when she sees that faraway look my eyes, for the call of a fish is difficult to accept by those who do not hear or understand it. I am not sure I can explain it myself. It may be a gift, or it could be a curse, depending on whose sense of values are being tested.

It's doubtful anyone really knows where and when it all began, but man's piscatorial quests probably had their origin back in the distant millennia when some hairy-knuckled Neanderthal waded into a shallow stream and tossed a flopping predecessor to a trout out on the bank.

More than likely he learned this by watching a grizzly doing it in much the same manner. Or, it's even possible he was the very first of our ancestors to use a tool, such as a pointed stick, to gig the scaly critter.

In doing so, this early humanoid may have even felt something besides a hunger pang – perchance a tiny spark of satisfaction in knowing he had outwitted his prey. The simple enjoyment alone may have encouraged him to repeat the act now and then, marking the beginning of his evolution from a food-seeking survivalist of prehistory and liking him to the sporting angler of the present.

It is possible all of this has filtered down through thousands of generations to find a home in my own genes where it spawned the challenging call of a fish that I hear today.

Then again, hearing the call could have been inherited from a later and more intelligent form of mankind. A dreamer, perhaps, who, while looking at the sunsets, the rainbows, the mountains, and the flowing streams, felt a kinship with the natural world around him.

Could it be this early relative came to love the aesthetic beauty of the environs surrounding the waters where fishes dwell? And, could it be the passions of this distant relative have dribbled down through the eons of blood and chromosomes until they linked up with me, bonding the two of us with the present?

A thousand times I have heard the fishes calling my name, and I have answered their beckoning whenever possible. As a lad, they came to me while gazing longingly from the schoolhouse window, only to be returned to my textbooks when a hickory pointer rapped my knuckles.

I heeded those calls in my youth, and I still do today. Furthermore, I have little doubt that in coming years, when lungs, sight and muscles shall fail, I am sure their biddings will continue to haunt me.

And, there is yet another call I hear in the spring. Like that of the fishes it comes from a source where no sound is expected, and again, it seems to be heard only by those of us who dream. Hence, the skepticism of the dubious ones who do not.

I hear it on bright sunny days when the woodlands begin to warm following winter's thaw. These calls come to me from yellow morels as they appear mysteriously overnight in the still moist woodlands and around the decaying stumps of slippery elms. That's when I hear them inviting me to come play their game of hide-and-seek as they conceal themselves in the shadows of weeds and wild plants and beneath the leaves of May-apples.

"I'm beginning to wonder what kind of a ding-a-ling I married," says Pet. "Claiming you hear a fish calling you is ridiculous enough, but a call coming from fungi? The very suggestion is downright idiotic.

"I do believe you have reached a point in life when you are in urgent need of psychiatric help, and I'm just the one who can dispense it.

"The very next time you start this irrational gibberish with me, I'll tell you exactly what sound you will be hearing. It will be the gurgling 'Good-bye' coming from that bourbon and scotch in your liquor cabinet being poured down the drain."

GROWING UP WITH YOUR KIDS

"Dad, when are you going to take me fishing in Canada?"

Mike's question should not have surprised me, but it did. In fact, it arrived with quite a jolt, hitting home loud and clear. He was growing up, and I was getting older.

When he was seven, I began taking him with me occasionally as I fished the strip pits and farm ponds near our home in southern Indiana. While I fished these local waters quite often, those times with Mike were not as often as I now wish they had been. He learned to cast with amazing accuracy for a little guy, and accumulated a number of bluegill, crappie, and a few small bass to his credit.

GROWING UP WITH YOUR KIDS

Until now, my annual treks to the North Country had always taken place with a few close fishing buddies. Over the years, I looked forward to those trips with that gang, and they became somewhat of a tradition each year. They were enthusiastically planned in the early spring, carried out in the summer, and relived again and again in our reminiscing at our gatherings during the long winter months.

Although he had said nothing before, Mike, evidently, had been closely observing and listening to all our stories with much interest and a quiet longing. But, it was not until he posed his question that I realized how important this had become.

So the following June found us settled in our comfortable cabin on the Little Canoe River in the Ontario bush country. We were thirty miles by water from the nearest town and with more than enough provisions for the two weeks we had planned to stay. It was just the two of us – a nervous dad, bent on making this special fishing trip with his son as successful as possible, and an excited youngster, who enjoyed every mile of the long drive from Indiana to the boarder crossing at International Falls.

Our first morning on the water was beautiful, and Mike's initial cast was rewarded with the slashing strike of a northern pike. His excitement was a picture I'll always remember. The battle, in which everything seemed to go wrong, somehow came to a triumphal conclusion, when eight pounds of saw-toothed, red-eyed fury finally ended up in the bottom of our boat.

Before the day was over, Mike had become a veteran pike fisherman, and we also took a couple of his keeper-size walleye back to the cabin for dinner that evening. It was as fine as any we ever tasted, and I'll always cherish the photo I took of that proud and happy youngster holding up his catch.

From that day on, it seemed Mike couldn't get in enough fishing hours.

The following morning, as we fished our way upstream, a doe and fawn watched us from a shallow bay, and later, we watched a beaver gnawing on a small birch at the water's edge while an eagle soared majestically, high over head. Mike asked a thousand questions, and I did my best to answer each of them with the knowledge and wisdom he expected from me.

At the northern reaches of the river, where a small rapid descends from the upper lakes, we beached our boat. With tackle in hand and day packs on our backs, we hiked across the quarter mile portage to where our canoe was stashed on the shore of another wilderness lake.

About halfway up the trail, Mike's excitement really peaked, when just ahead of us a young black bear scurried off the trail and into the forest.

Later that morning, as we were fishing in the mouth of a small bay, it was my own stupidity that lost a beautiful walleye for Mike. It was a good one, too – at least twelve or more pounds. He was playing it perfectly, but when he worked it in close, I made the mistake of trying to net it on the leeward side of the canoe.

The wind was rather strong that morning, and a sudden gust drifted us sideways over the fish just as I reached for it. In my awkward position, I snagged the lure's hooks on the outside of the net. That's all it took. The walleye was gone.

I have lost many nice sized fish over the years, but this one I regretted squandering most of all. And, it still bothers me. How I wanted to boat that walleye for my son.

While obviously disappointed, Mike must have sensed my helpless frustration.

"That's OK, Dad," he said, "We'll get another one."

Coming back down the river that evening, Mike asked if I would teach him how to run the boat. At first, I had him sit beside me on the stern seat. With his hand on the outboard's tiller alongside of mine, I let him feel the boat's response as we steered right and left and how twisting the throttle would speed us up or slow us down.

A couple of days later, I thought it was time he graduated to the next level. The motor was an 18 horsepower with a heavy compression, so I had to

14

pull the starter cord for him before I moved up to the bow seat. He closely followed my instructions and did a good job running the boat down the winding river and back to the cabin. After that, it became a daily routine for him to take the helm on our way in from fishing each evening.

One day after having our lunch at the cabin, Mike asked me if he could take the boat and fish up the river alone. He was looking me straight in the eye, and I could tell this was not just a spur-of-the-moment idea. He was serious, and it was apparently important to him. The question awaited an immediate response, and it was up to me.

From the cabin, it is only about three miles upstream to the portage, and there was no way he could become lost. I replaced the big motor with our spare 6 horsepower. It was large enough to move our heavy sixteen foot boat, but there was no need to worry about sudden accelerations or high speeds.

Mike arranged his fishing tackle in the boat and started the motor. I untied the bow rope and pushed him away from the dock. He shifted into forward, and as he waved to me, he wore a smile I'll never forget. I stood there on the dock listening to the fading drone of the kicker long after he had passed out of sight around the first bend.

Returning to the cabin, I tried to catch up on my writing, but was having trouble concentrating on my work. I kept looking at my watch about every five minutes. An hour passed - then two.

Twice I walked down to the dock and listened for the sound of the outboard, but heard nothing. I thought about taking the canoe and going to look for him, but talked myself out of it.

Accomplishing this on his own must have meant a lot to my son. He wanted to show me he was growing up and could be trusted at doing a man's thing. It would have been wrong to spoil that for him.

By the time the third hour passed, I was about to go out of my gourd, imagining all sorts of trouble he could be having. Suppose he had sheared a pin or had broken the prop on a rock. It would be a long row back to the cabin for him. Maybe he had beached the boat to walk across the portage. There was no telling what he could have run into on the trail. Perhaps he had hooked himself with a lure or worse yet, maybe he had fallen overboard trying to start the motor.

Pacing back and forth on the dock, I was just before jumping in the canoe and heading out, when I heard the faint sound of a distant outboard. I ran back up the path to the front porch of the cabin. Plopping down in a chair, I faked reading a book.

Mike finally rounded the bend and waved to me as he slowly steered the boat toward the dock. Acting as nonchalant as possible, I took my time strolling down to the dock, stopping along the way to throw a small twig from the path. When I tied off his bow line, I noticed a fair-sized northern pike lying in the net in the bottom of the boat.

"I caught three smaller ones and turned them loose," said Mike, "But this one swallowed my spinner, and I couldn't get the hook out. That's why I came back so soon."

We had his pike for dinner that evening.

In the days that followed, we enjoyed our fishing together more and more. On our last afternoon before leaving for home, Mike tied into a four pound plus, tail-walking, smallmouth bass that really gave him fits. My netting it for him kind of made up for my clumsy loss of his big walleye.

After dinner, in the silence of the evening, we sat on the boat dock and experienced a Canadian sunset as beautiful as any I have ever seen. From out on the lake, near the mouth of the river, the cry of a loon echoed across the waters.

Later, after darkness had set in, we were treated to an awesome panoramic spectacle in the northern sky. As we watched, the Aurora's display reflected in the water. Pink, curtains hung in folds and rolled across the heavens, only to change into long, green rays streaking upward as if trying to pierce the great beyond.

Our trip together that year was just the beginning of many memory filled years for our whole family. With each summer that followed, Pet and I found ourselves growing up with our kids at our cabin on the Little Canoe. At the time, we failed to realize how precious those days would become for us all.

Before we realized it, Mike, Kathy and Connie were married and gone, with families of their own. Now, scattered as they are, their schedules seem to always be in conflict. Getting everyone together for a family Christmas is difficult enough. Planning summer vacations together in Canada is impossible.

As the years go by, those wonderful times have become more and more precious. They were packed with experiences we will never forget. Of all the things our kids learned from those summers on the Little Canoe, perhaps the most important is how they should make the most of every moment they have with their own children, for each wonderful day together will pass all too quickly.

THE PISCATORIAL PADRÉ AND OL' SCOW

The Padré was a true "man of the cloth" and as devoted to his church and its creeds as was his boss in the Vatican. He was completely dedicated to his calling in every way with the exception of his leaning toward two secular distractions: He had a passion for the piscatorial sport, and he was known to have a taste for an occasional dram of "the creature".

More than a few of his holier-than-thou parishioners frowned upon such irreverent delinquencies and openly voiced their objections, claiming such carrying on would lead to no good.

"The fishing and imbibing are bad enough," they emphasized, "but associating with such an unscrupulous character as Ol' Scow is downright scandalous if not sacrilegious."

THE PISCATORIAL PADRÉ AND OL' SCOW

"Why do you cast these self-righteous stones?" asked the priest, challenging their sinful allegations. "Do we not use the vintage of the grapes in celebrating Holy Mass everyday? And you surely realize that wasn't iced tea the Apostles were sipping at the Last Supper."

Then, as an afterthought, he added, "...and were not the Apostles also fishermen?

"As for Ol' Scow, well... He's just a sheep of a different flock, you might say."

The Padré's fondness for angling was founded more in the quest itself than it was in the actual catch. To him, his love of the outdoors and all its wonders was like being in a great cathedral with an azure sky and a few scattered clouds for its frescoed dome. The velvet sound of rippling waters and soft breezes among the pines were as whispered vespers, and his music was provided by a choir of songbirds.

The sweet aroma of blooming wild flowers was his incense, and the wild creatures of the woods and waters made up the congregation of this, his second parish. Here, he could inhale the clean, freshness of nature that offered a peaceful sanctuary for his meditations the likes of which he found in but few other places.

In comparison, the good Padré's favorite fishing companion, Ol' Scow, was of an entirely different world. He was an ornery, blasphemous cuss with an unequaled vocabulary of obscene adjectives, and he was a character of somewhat doubtful morals.

How these two opposites ever got together in the first place no one quite seems to remember, but their association prompted a wide array of speculation and wagering on its dubious outcome.

Scow had spent most of his life bumming around the Sabine River area on the Texas/Louisiana border where he hunted, fished, and trapped while acquiring a well-earned reputation for his boozing, brawling, and possible banditry. All of which was probably true at one time or another.

That is it was until an almost forgotten and long estranged aunt passed away leaving her entire estate to her only living relative.

Among the many assets in the highly valued bequest was a rather lucrative soft drink bottling business in a Midwest city that, just by chance, was also the home of the Padré's parish.

This legacy, and a strongly suggested piece of advise from a local sheriff, prompted Ol' Scow to give up his meager holdings in Texas and move north to become a successful, although still a somewhat raunchy, business man.

Like the Padré, Ol' Scow also had a following that took issue with his choice of fishing buddies. It was the unanimous opinion of the brotherhood of freeloaders, at Ike's Booze & Billiard

Emporium, that such a fraternization was definitely one big mistake.

"That there preacher feller will be changin' yer way of thinkin'", they warned, fearing more than anything the potential loss of Scow's nightly habit of buying drinks for the house.

"Oh, the Padré's OK," Scow assured them. "He's jist kinda sot in his ways. He jaws to hisself a lot in some furin' lingo, but ya'll don't need to stew 'bout me.

"I'll guaran-damn-tee ya, he's shor's hell ain't gonna plant his snare hooks in this here ol' coon-ass."

However, even with the most sincere pledges from the pair, the Padré's communicants and Scow's boozing sidekicks were not at all convinced. In fact, these two, normally contradicting, factions were, for once, in total agreement: "It's definitely not good.

"One of these days," they predicted, "whichever way it goes, and for better or worse, one of these two is sure to contaminate the other."

Nevertheless, the Padré and Ol' Scow continued to enjoy their angling and companionship with no visible sign of any influence being exchanged – at least, for the time being.

Saturdays seemed to be their mutual choice of fishing days, and they seldom missed a weekend as long as the weather cooperated. Their time of day worked out pretty well, too. As pastor of St. Simon Peter's, the Padré scheduled himself for celebrating early Mass each Saturday morning. This left the rest of his day free for fishing.

Then, too, since Ol' Scow wasn't much for yakking while in the boat, except for his outburst of profanity when things didn't go exactly right, it afforded the Padré ample opportunity to ponder on the subject of his up-and-coming Sunday morning sermon.

On the other hand, Ol' Scow's soft drink business was an automated operation with its bottling line working five days a week. When his employees flipped the switch on Friday evening, everything was shut down for the weekend. This left the door open for him to pursue his angling pastime.

So, early each Saturday morning, while the Padré was busy with his religious duties, Scow would slip down to the bottling plant and pour a couple of ounces of his favorite Kentucky bourbon in the first six bottles coming up on the line. Then he would flip the "Start" switch.

By the time he and the Padré arrived at the boat launching ramp, those capped bottles of spiked soda were well chilled in their iced-down cooler.

Their weekly fishing jaunts continued for a couple of years with no visible changes taking place in either of their personalities. It was only then the Padré's church-going followers and Ol' Scow's bar-fly friends began to breathe a tad easier. So far, their concerns appeared to be unfounded, and everything seemed to be working out much better than they had anticipated.

Then, one memorable Saturday morning, as the Padré was casting and retrieving his lure along the edge of a large bed of water lilies, the surface suddenly swelled in one, huge, boiling eruption. His casting rod bowed and threatened to break when it was yanked down hard against the boat's gunwale.

Whatever that heavy thing was at the end of the Padré's line, it streaked away, under the lily pads, in one direction, while at the same time, the priest reared back in the other. Several of the pads folded up and disappeared beneath the surface as the heavy casting line became hopelessly entangled in the jungle of underwater vegetation. A stand-off followed with both man and fish being anchored solidly to the unyielding plants.

Ol' Scow tried to help by leaning far out over the side and reaching down in the water as far as he could. Grasping the lilies by the stems, he pulled the heavy johnboat through the pads. As he was tugging on one, it suddenly broke, and at the same time so did the line.

Within arm's reach of the boat, a humongous fish shot clear of the water. The hooks of the Padré's lure were embedded in its upper lip with a foot of the broken casting line still attached.

It was like watching a slow-motion movie film. There, suspended in mid-air before their very eyes was what had to be a record-breaking bass of unbelievable proportions. The huge critter seemed to just hang there for one, long, gut-wrenching moment. Finally, when it splashed down, it sent a geyser of water upward, drenching the two awe-stricken fishermen and the resulting waves rocked their boat.

"GOD ALMIGHTY, DAMN!" roared the Padré. "DID YOU SEE THE ----ING SHOULDERS ON THAT SON OF A B_ _ _ _?"

"BENEDICTAMUS DOMINO!" gasped Ol' Scow, crossing himself.

Stunned by the entire incident and personally embarrassed by their own outbursts, the two just sat there, red-faced and staring at each other in the awkward silence of disbelief.

Finally, when he had regained his composure, it was the Padré who cleared his throat, and in a cool, calm voice broke the spell.

"Scow, I do believe perhaps it's about time you and I had a couple of those special sodas of yours."

THE OLD COW POND

"I've got it all figgered out," said Duffy Patterson III. "We can stash our bikes in the ditch by the fence an' slip in the back way."

"It won't work," I argued.

"Will too," insisted Duffy, hunkering down to trace out his plan in the sand. "All we gotta do is split up, see? You an' Jimmy can keep the bull busy down at the south end of the pasture while the rest of us duck across up at this end. We can make it to the other side an' be through the barb' wire fore Ol' Killer can get back at us."

"Yeah... but how 'bout me an' Jimmy?"

"Don't ya see, Dummy? When that ol' bull comes after us, you two can shag it cross down at your end," explained Duffy, beaming at his own genius.

THE OLD COW POND

"I don't know. You forgettin' 'bout Ol' Muggs? How 'bout him? He'll shoot us fer sure, if he catches us in there. That's what he'll do."

"No he won't," growled Duffy, standing up and throwing his tracing stick away. "I heard him tell Pa he was goin' up to Rockville to do some dickerin' for an ol' tractor. I bet he won't be back 'til after dark. So let's get goin'."

Muggs McGlone's cow pond was reputedly the very best place to fish in the whole world. Every kid in the county knew that for sure. The only problem was the place was posted: "KEEP OUT — NO FISHING — NO HUNTING — THIS MEANS YOU!"

These orders were notoriously enforced by McGlone and his 12 guage double barrel, his dog, Savage, and Killer, his bull.

We had all heard the many hair-raising legends of what happened to young poachers who tried sneaking into the forbidden cow pond.

"...an' his Ma an' Pa was so scare't, they moved away the very nex' day. That's the truth, too. The kid what tolt me crossed his heart an' hoped to die."

While such tales spawned sheer terror in youthful imaginations, for some of us, the challenge to fish in Muggs McGlone's cow pond became more of an obsession than just a mere desire. This was especially so with Duffy Patterson III.

28

THE OLD COW POND

Somehow Duffy was always the self-appointed leader of our band of barefoot urchins. He was also the one who concocted most of the schemes that resulted in our getting in trouble, which was nearly a daily occurrence.

On this particular summer day we were lazing around, sunning ourselves on a sandbar after a refreshing swim in our favorite hole near the old covered bridge. That's when Duffy was suddenly nudged by the latest of his brilliant notions: "Let's go fish the Ol' Cow Pond."

As usual, Duffy's well-engineered plan appeared to be flawless – at least in the beginning. When our bikes were hidden in the weeds along the road bordering the McGlone Farm, Jimmy and I ran along on our side of the barbed wire fence, shouting and waving our willow fishing poles. Sure enough, that snorting mountain of red-eyed fury, known as "Killer", came thundering our way, madder than a wet hornet.

At the same time, Duffy, Sam, Whitey, and Bill started whooping it up as they hightailed it across the upper end of the pasture. In a cloud of dust, Killer skidded to a change in direction as he headed for his new tormentors in an earth shaking charge. Then it was our turn.

"When we get to the fence, hold up the wire for me, Jimmy, I yelled. Mom said if I tore my new overalls, she'd tan my hide."

THE OLD COW POND

Duffy and the others were through the fence on the far side of the pasture before the bull was half way there, but, Jimmy and I still had a good ten yards to go when Killer swapped ends again, heading back for us a full speed.

"Whee ma-ha-ade hit!" I gasped, when we joined our pals.

"Yee-yeah," panted Jimmy, "bu-but ya ripped the leg of your new bibs divin' through the fence. Your ma's gonna give ya a thumpin',"

"Here," said Duffy, handing me his Barlow knife. "All ya gotta do is cut a few inches off the bottom of each leg, an' she'll never notice it."

"Yeah, agreed Bill. "She'll jest think you're growin' kinda fast."

The fishing that day in the cow pond proved to be somewhat on the sluggish side. In fact, it was late in the afternoon before Duffy came up with our first catch - a six inch bluegill.

"Thought this was 'posed to be sich a good fishing' hole," grumbled Whitey.

"It is," said Duffy. "Can't ya see they're jest starting' to bite? Everyone knows this is the best time-a-day for fishing'. Why, I'll bet we'll..."

BOOM!!!

A string of number eight bird shot rattled through the tree tops high over our heads.

"HEY! YA LI'L BASTARDS, GET YER PIMPLY ASSES OUTA HERE AFORE I BLASTS "EM!!!" yelled Muggs McGlone as he and his dog, Savage, topped the knoll overlooking the cow pond.

In wild-eyed panic, we abandoned everything – fishing poles, worm cans, and various pieces of clothing not immediately attached. We tripped and stumbled in a mad and frenzied retreat.

The shortest way out was the way we had come in, and the barbed wire didn't even slow us down. Over, under, and through it we scrambled in our frantic dash to get across the pasture.

My hip pocket and a good sized piece of denim from the seat of my new bibs were left hanging on the fence. Not a thought was wasted on the bull, as the immediate terror of being blasted into eternity by Muggs McGlone dominated everything else.

"BOOM!!!"

Thankfully McGlone's shootin' eye must have been way off that day, for the second barrel of his scatter gun carried the shot whistling above us higher than the first, but it succeeded in speeding up our hysterical flight even more. Fortunately, the blast also saved us from Ol' Killer, as it sent the frightened bull stampeding off in the opposite direction.

Just before reaching the fence on the freedom side of the pasture, I tripped, doing a belly-slider through a pile of fresh cow chips, but it didn't slow me, and I caught up with the others as they reached the fence. Those last strands of wire were negotiated much like the first, leaving pieces of torn shirts and additional strips of denim decorating the barbs.

Our bicycles were retrieved from the ditch without our even losing a stride, and the McGlone Farm was left in the distance as we raced down the gravel road at break-neck speed. A good half-mile from the scene of our near demise, our frantic pedaling finally came to a halt. We were completely pooped out.

Covered with sweat and road dust, we were draped over our bicycle handlebars, exhausted and gasping for breath.

"Wh-wh-WOW!!! TH-that wa-wa-was close," wheezed Bill.

"Hi-hi-I to-tolt ya wheee could ma-make hhhit wh-wh-whid out getting' caught," choked Duffy.

"Ye-Yeah," panted Jimmy, "b-but hhI think hhI've ha-had 'nuff fishin' fer a-a-while."

"M-m-meee, too," was the huffed and unanimous agreement.

"Tell ya what," said Duffy, once we had recouped and were heading for home, "tomorrow, let's forget 'bout the fishin' an' go explorin' in Wolf Cave. Maybe we'll find a hidden treasure or somethin'."

"But we'll get lost in there an' never find our way out in the dark," I protested.

"Won't either," frowned Duffy.

"Will too."

"No we won't. I got it all figgered out. We'll jest unwind a kite string when we go in, see? Then all we gotta do is..."

"Hi, Mom. Hi, Dad," I greeted, slamming the screen door as I entered the kitchen.

"Well, it's about time you came home. Supper is getting cold, and I've been calling... What in the world...? What's the odor??? What have you...?

"Young man, get yourself washed up and into some clean clothes, and I mean NOW!!! Take what's left of those smelly old overalls out to the trash burner.

"Where have you been anyway?"

"Been fishin', Ma," I answered.

"That reminds me," said Dad, "I saw Muggs McGlone in town the other day – we went to grade school together, you know. He's a bit of an eccentric old... well anyway, I was telling him how much you like to fish, and he said if you wanted to come out to his farm someday, he'd take you back to his cow pond and let you try your luck. He said it's loaded with big bluegill."

"Yeah, Dad. That's great. Oh, by the way, would you mind if I borrow your flash light tomorrow?"

THE SONGS OF A STRIPPER

The slow, bump and grind music and the songs of sirens drift through open doorways of gaudily lighted honky-tonks on a humid, summer evening. In cities throughout the world, aimless souls and hopeless derelicts stagger from one strip pit to another in search of whatever consolation they may find to ease the pains of broken promises and lost loves. The drama is a sad but nightly occurrence and as ageless as it is common.

On the same sultry evening in southern Indiana, another song is heard reverberating from a strip pit of a different nature.

"BURR-UMP," it echoes from the shadows on a far shore and down a long, narrow arm of calm, dark water.

"BURR-UMP-UMP-UMP," the ballad is taken up by a trio of songsters.

THE SONGS OF A STRIPPER

From the high-banked shoreline, the repeated accompaniment of an owl's "WHO... WHO... WHO-WHOOOO!" and the rhythmical voice of a whippoorwill join the chorus of the bull frogs. These are the night songs emanating from the strip pits in my world, and I am as attracted to them, as are those human wrecks of the neon ghettos are to the gin mills they frequent.

My kind of "stripper" is the bastard child of a land raped years ago by coal mining companies. In its adolescent years, conservation laws forced the rapers to cover its ugly, barren spill banks, of clay, rock and shale, with the greenery of pine trees. Now, in its adulthood, its deep spring fed waters are nestled between the high, forested mounds. On this night, the concert of the wild ones add to the unique attraction I find in my kind of strip pit.

By nature, man is not a night creature. Like some animal species, when the sun goes down, he will head for his lair and hole up until daylight. However, there are exceptions. Known as night-fishermen, we are considered by some to be of doubtful mentality, for we, too, have been seduced by the songs of a stripper.

In the summer months, the heat and brilliance of a high sun will drive the fish to shaded cover and cooler depths. It is then that much of their feeding will take place between sunset and dawn. For fish and fishermen alike, these later hours are a pleasant relief from the sweltering temperatures of the day.

Now the strip pit becomes even more picturesque as it is viewed in the serene glow of moonlight. Scenes familiar to anglers during the day, present an entirely different picture on such evenings. In darker lunar periods, the shadows and reflections will change the perspective yet again.

Personally, I have found night-fishing to be an intriguing sport regardless of the lighting conditions. Over the years, I have spent many late hours casting into the shadows of the high spill banks bordering the placid waters of strip pits. To me, the exciting eruption of a striking bass, shattering the dead silence of a dark night, can only be compared to the flush of a covey of quail from under a hunter's feet. There is nothing quite like it, and the thrill is difficult to explain.

Picture yourself in a shallow draft johnboat, drifting slowly on the dark waters of a strip pit. A few stars in the midnight canopy reflect in the mirrored calm. The shoreline is obscured in the shadows cast by the high spill-banks surrounding you. The only sound is the soft "slurp" of a surface-feeding bluegill or the occasional "BURRR-UMP" of a bullfrog from somewhere down the long narrow lake.

THE SONGS OF A STRIPPER

Respecting the silence, you and your fishing buddy have not uttered a word in more than half and hour, but you welcome the company of his silhouette on the boat's stern seat. The slow, hushed stroke of his sculling paddle moves the boat a few yards farther without disturbing the quiet surface.

You are conscious of the surrounding darkness, and you experience the uneasy feeling that you are somewhat out of your element. Perhaps it is a throwback to a time when ancient superstitions were often connected with the night.

You lob your surface-popping plug into the blackness, blindly feeling for the invisible shoreline. You are relieved when you hear a soft splash, an indication that your cast has found water. Silence would have meant you had overshot your mark, and your lure had disappeared somewhere in the brush high on the bank.

You let the lure rest without movement, as you slowly and quietly reel up the slack line. After what seems an eternity, you snap you wrist back, flipping your rod tip upward.

"PLUNK!"

You see the rippling rings spreading outward, marring the calm, dark water where your unseen popper floats. You let it rest again, slowly counting to yourself, "One... two... three... four... five..."

Ever so gently you twitch the rod tip a second time, and hear a softer

"plunk". Once again the spreading rings die away, and the lure lies motionless as you resume your count, "One... two... th..."
   "POW!"
The lake suddenly explodes, raping the stillness of the night. Your nerves become liquid. Your stomach turns over. Instinctively, you rear back, jerking the rod tip upward. Immediately, it is yanked back down by the furious counteraction from an unknown force at the other end of your line.

Your breath is jammed somewhere between your throat and your lungs. It takes place all at once in a single, overpowering drama that freezes motion and time as well as your spine.

Your bent rod is pulled around the boat's bow, and you hold it high over your head, twisting in your seat, as your line slices out of the dark shadows and into the slightly brighter water in the center of the strip pit. Here, the surface erupts again, belching forth six pounds of uncoiling, head shaking furor that drops back into the lake, sending up a gusher of water.

With the applied pressure of your arched rod, the line curves in an arc slicing a "V" on the surface pointing directly toward the boat. You desperately crank your reel, trying to pick up slack line. Now, the upper half of your rod bends over the gunwale and down under the boat. Quickly, you thrust your arms over the side and deep in the water to keep the rod from breaking. The bass leaps again, closer this time, dousing you and your fishing buddy as it crashes back into the water.

Twice more you bring the fish near. Twice again it darts away to deeper, darker climes, but the continuous pressure of the arched rod and tight line begins to take its toll. On a slower pass beside the boat, your partner slips his net under the bass, finalizing the conflict.

Your heart is pounding, your mouth full of cotton, and your hands quiver as you remove the hook from the gaping maw. Three more times, you will experience a near coronary before the night is over. Your fishing buddy will top your count by two.

In the early morning of another day, I visit the stripper alone. The sounds of the night have fallen silent, and the dawn bathes the scene in gold. As this fades with the higher sun, the water takes on the reflections of an azure sky. Now, the songs of my stripper are of a different melody.

The "cheeping" is that of a cardinal flitting among the spill-bank pines. The soft rustle of water comes from a raccoon washing his crayfish breakfast near the cattails. And, with a sucking smack of a feeding bluegill, an insect disappears from the lake's surface.

I quietly paddle my johnboat down the narrow gorge. In a shallow, pad-covered bay at the far end of the strip pit, a shaft of sunlight filters through the pines to fall on the bloom of a water lily. Droplets of dew on the delicate petals glisten like diamonds.

I paddle the boat to within casting distance of the lilies. My small, fly rod popper is well placed in a pocket of open water amid the green pads. It rests high on the surface, and twitching the rod tip causes the cork bug to curtsy just enough, to produce a faint, but widening, ripple. When it subsides, my hand tightens on the rod's grip to repeat the action, but my movement is interrupted by a sudden upheaval of water, lily pads, popper and largemouth bass.

The peace and serenity of the stripper's morning is immediately shattered. There is a tumbling of rock and a sliding of shale, as a heretofore unobserved, but now startled, deer scrambles up and over the top of the spill-bank. Several frogs splash into the water as they dive from shoreline perches. With an alarmed, "QUAAACK" and a pounding of wing beats, a brace of mallards jump from the reeds.

The bass clears the surface again in a tail flipping, end-over-end vault and then makes the mistake of heading away from the pads toward the open, deeper water. The fight is now on my terms and short lived. I heft it by the lower lip and pluck my popper from its mouth. The fish is a healthy specimen of three pounds - plus or minus and ounce or two. As I gently return it to the stripper, I recall someone once saying, "You don't catch fish in a strip pit . . . you mine them."

Later, after moving the boat down the lake, a smaller popper rewards me with a half dozen nice bluegill. Their resistance to my light action fly rod is exciting, and their uniform size is ideal for the skillet.

By now, the sun has climbed to its midday perch. Activities cease, and all is quiet once again. The increased heat and direct, overhead light urge fish and wild things alike to seek rest in secluded places once more. The thought is receptive to man as well.

About four in the afternoon, signs of life slowly return to the stripper. As I step from the cabin, following a relaxing nap and a few chapters of a good book, the "SLURP" of a feeding bluegill is heard. From the boat dock, where the sun still shines bright and warm, a plunge into the blue waters revives me from a sleepy sluggishness.

My swim is pleasant, as I experience the feeling of a oneness with all that surrounds me, and I become an intricate part of the strip pit. The wild things, the fishes and I are all brothers, sharing the same habitat.

I swim slowly about. I tread water. Then, I dive to be closer to my kin who dwell in the deep. Several feet down, the water is dark and icy cold, taking my breath away. I quickly return to the surface, gasping for air, and I realize that the world of a stripper can never be intimately shared by humans, but only observed.

By now the sun is low and the pit is once again bathed in color – a richer, deeper gold than that of early morning. Gradually, the western sky changes to red, gracing the spill banks with rosy hues, and a long path of crimson streaks across the water from the fireball sinking behind the spill banks.

As darkness returns, so does the evening's overture. The sounds of the night return, and the combined voices of crickets, locusts, katydids, owls and the bull frogs are once again blended in the songs of a stripper.

"YOU SAY YOU STEPPED IN WHAT?"

Five o'clock – cocktail time – I entered BJ's Rod & Gun Club, and as expected, found The Judge perched on his favorite bar stool, swizzling his bourbon and branch.

"Well! Look who made it home," he greeted. "I hear you had an interesting trip."

"Yeah, interesting! We're lucky to have made it back at all."

"I haven't heard about it," said BJ, leaning across the bar. "What happened?"

"You wouldn't believe me if I told you," I responded, hoping to be pressed into narrating the details of our tarpon and snook fishing trek to Costa Rica.

"So why don't you try us anyway?" said The Judge with a "ho-hum" sigh.

"YOU SAY YOU STEPPED IN WHAT?"

"Well, because of delays and cancellations, and waiting on standby, and rescheduled flights, and lost luggage on each of the three airlines, and several hours of arguing with Costa Rican Customs, we were a day and a half late in getting to our fishing camp.

"But once we arrived everything was great. The scenery was beautiful, – our accommodations, the food, the fishing, the people we met – it was all terrific... except for what happened on the third day we were there.

"That's when we upset our boat in the ocean just outside the mouth of the river, and the place was full of sharks, and..."

"WHOA... WHOA... WHOA... Slow it down a notch or two," interrupted His Honor, "Now let's get this straight.

"You say you stepped in WHAT?"

I ignored The Judge's snide remark. By now, several of the Rod & Gun Club's regulars had gathered around to hear about our adventure.

As I continued with my story, I vividly pictured everything that had taken place: From late January through early May, the rivers, lagoons and off-shore waters of Costa Rica are teeming with tarpon. But, this was October.

It was the best time for snook – big snook – and that is why we had come.

In the late afternoon of our arrival, my buddy, "Catfish" Ennis and I boated a pair of fine snook while fishing the lagoon within sight of our

villa.   Each weighed in excess of
eighteen pounds.

In waters we had previously fished,
a 15 pounder would be considered a
trophy worthy of mounting.   But here,
the two we brought to the dock received
nothing more than a nod and the casual,
"Good, just right to feed the camp this
evening."

While   snook   were   the   primary
objectives   of   this   trip,   the
possibility of lucking into a tarpon
kept our adrenalin simmering on hold
just below the boiling point.

During our first two days of
fishing, we made contact with a few of
those big, silver critters, but each
time, following a series of picturesque
jumps, our lures were launched into
space.

One morning, while fishing in the
delta of a little river several miles
from camp, I managed to plant a barb in
the jaws of a small tarpon.   After a
couple of exciting, end-over-end
vaults, I thought I had him, but it was
not to be.

The fish suddenly took off in a
panic-stricken dash for freedom in the
open sea beyond the breakers.   There
was good reason for his doing so, too,
but he didn't make it.   Centered in a
huge boil on the surface, a smashing
jolt nearly yanked the rod from my
hands. Then the line went limp. All I
reeled in was the tarpon's head.   A
large shark had severed its body just
behind its gill covers.

"YOU SAY YOU STEPPED IN WHAT?"

The next day, we were fishing in the calm water of a lagoon inside the mouth of the Parismena River where it emptied into the Caribbean near our camp. We had two 16 mm movie cameras with us hoping to film some dramatic action scenes while doing battle with the leaping tarpon.

There were plenty of snook in the river that morning, but out beyond its mouth, in the open sea, we spotted a large concentration of big tarpon. Apparently, they were feeding on a school of bait fish, for they were rolling on the surface and leaping clear out of the water. The scene was enough to drive any fishing nut out of his gourd, and that's exactly the effect it had on us.

It was kind of like flipping a light switch. We turned off our very last amperage of rational thinking and leaned heavily on outright stupidity.

Our johnboat was a heavy, 18 foot, flat-bottomed river model of the type used by commercial fishermen for raising their big nets. It had 20 inches of freeboard and an extra wide beam making it very stable. Enough so that we could stand and walk around without danger of tipping it. For fishing in the sluggish jungle streams and quiet lagoons, it was ideal, but it was definitely not built for going out to sea.

However, watching those airborne tarpon was simply too much of a challenge. With all of our smarts placed on hold, and over the objections of Juan, our guide, we finally talked him into taking us out into the open water of the Caribbean.

Where the outgoing river current meets the incoming surf, the water is always turbulent. But, with a favorable, off-shore wind, as we had that day, we made it easily through the river's mouth and out into the gentle rise and fall of the rolling swells.

About a quarter of a mile out, we began trolling parallel to the shoreline. Occasionally, a tarpon would strike a lure, only to fling it back at us when reaching the peak of a spectacular jump. Every now and then, we would see the dorsal fin of a large black shark slicing the surface within a few yards of us. Comparing one with the boat's length, I estimated it to be at least 12 feet long, and as it cruised by, it rolled on its side enough to eye-ball us before disappearing. He was so close; I could have actually touched him.

It was later in the afternoon, when we were so deeply engrossed in our quest to film a leaping tarpon; we failed to notice the changes taking place around us.

The wind had now shifted to an on-shore direction, and the swells were much larger with scattered whitecaps flashing in the tropical sun. The surf was now crashing heavily on the beach, and at Juan's insistence, we left the tarpon and headed for the calm waters of the lagoon.

With his hand on the tiller, our guide's concerned eyes were fixed on the rampaging water in the mouth of the river. So to help raise the bow and better distribute our weight, Ennis and I moved to a rear seat where we sat facing Juan.

By the time we got into the raging turbulence, we were really flying, propelled like a surfer on a giant breaker. Ahead of us, the outgoing current was compressing the incoming rollers slowing our forward movement and leaving us caught in the curl of that huge wave building up behind us.

Suddenly, the blunt bow of our flat-bottomed johnboat plowed into the backside of the wave ahead. It was as if we had hit a brick wall. We came to a jarring halt, and that's all it took. The stern was lifted high, flipping us end-over-end. I saw Juan being catapulted over my head, and the boat was slammed upside down, as that massive breaker came crashing over us.

In desperation, I grabbed for the first thing in reach. It turned out to be the bow rope that was coiled on the seat beside me, and as I sank beneath our capsized boat, I was clinging to it like a bell ringer in a cathedral.

Water filled my ears and blurred my vision, and my world immediately changed to one of silence in the eerie green of sun-filtered sea water. The scream of the revving outboard motor, the roar of the surf, and the voice of Jack Ennis yelling, "HERE WE GO!" were immediately replaced by a soft gurgling sound in my ears.

Strange as it may seem, I felt no panic, just extreme anguish at myself for being so stupid and getting into this mess.

"You idiot," I thought. "How could you let yourself..."

The rope straightened out, and my feet touched the silt on the bottom of the delta. The water was only about twelve feet deep, and I pushed off as hard as I could, coming up under our overturned boat. Its flotation chambers prevented it from sinking, but the pounding waves kept shoving it down, and no air was trapped under it. By now, my lungs were aching.

"Got to – get some air... NOW!" I was beginning to panic. Dropping the rope, I grabbed the inverted boat gunwale with both hands pulling myself out and up from under my entrapment. When I broke the surface, I was choking and gasping for air. Ennis and Juan were already lying on the bottom of the capsized boat with their hands reaching out to pull me up with them.

The boat was still being pushed rapidly forward by the incoming waves, and my grip was slipping along the gunwale. I was being swept toward the stern. Our outboard motor had conked out when we flipped, and its shaft was sticking straight out behind the transom. When I lost my grip on the boat, I grabbed hold of the motor's lower unit just above the prop.

Now, I was being pulled along behind the boat as we were shooting into the mouth of the river. It was then a sudden and terrorizing thought struck me.

"OH, MY GOD! THOSE SHARKS! THIS DAMNED PLACE IS LOADED WITH 'EM, AND I'M BEING TROLLED LIKE LIVE BAIT!"

With an unknown strength, spawned of a desperate situation, I pulled myself up along the motor's shaft and onto the boat with Ennis and Juan.

Fortunately for us, two fishermen and their guide had witnessed the whole fiasco from a distance. Immediately, they left the peaceful water in the lagoon and raced their boat into the mouth of the river to pick us up.

Soon, we were standing on the beach, trembling on rubbery legs. Our nerves were shot – emotions completely out of control. We cheered, we cried, we laughed, and we pounded each other on the back. All our gear was lost – cameras, film, fishing tackle, the whole works, but somehow, thanks to no gifted wisdom of our own, we were alive and safe.

The seriousness of the traumatic episode didn't fully sink in until later that evening. We joined the people from the nearby village as they gathered around a driftwood fire on the beach near the mouth of the river. It was a beautiful night, and we were all having a great time.

"YOU SAY YOU STEPPED IN WHAT?"

The food and drinks were delicious and everyone was singing and dancing around when someone produced a long, nylon rope tipped with a wire leader and a big shark hook baited with a hunk of rotting snook meat. The rig was then hurled out into the river's mouth where our boat had upset a few hours earlier. Soon a game of "tug-o-war" took place with a gang of us on one end of the rope and an eleven foot shark on the other. The shark lost, and as it lay floundering in the sand, Ennis and I stood looking down at that gaping mouth of large, razor-sharp teeth. Then we looked at each other. Not a word was exchanged, nor was one needed.

At BJ's Rod & Gun Club, a dead silence prevailed as I ended my story with, "Well, I guess that's about it."

"THAT'S ABOUT IT?" roared The Judge. "You mean you've taken up most of our cocktail hour telling us how utterly stupid you two idiots were and you end it all with, 'THAT'S ABOUT IT?'

"This court's ruling is, "You now owe us all a round of drinks."

A jury of voices belted out its full agreement with His Honor's ruling, and BJ was already setting up the glasses.

INUKSOOK
(Symbols of Man)

In silent vigil they stand, just as they have for hundreds of years, ever since they were first placed there by the Inuit (Eskimos) to show that this is a "good place" and that man has been here.

High on the ridges overlooking Hudson Bay, where the Kovik River flows from Quebec's Ungava Peninsula, stand the Inuksook (Symbols of Man). Although they are nothing more than chunks and slabs of broken stone piled one upon another, from a distance they may easily be taken for people, sky-lined on the crests of the endless horizon. Worn and cracked by centuries of arctic weather, they are covered with lichen, and there is good reason for their being here.

INUKSOOK

Since the dawning of creation, man has been building statues of stone. Some were constructed as idols to be worshipped, some as art objects to be admired, and the meaningful explanation of others has long since been lost in antiquity. But, the Inuksook of the Inuit were built for the most basic reason of all – survival.

The Arctic Barrens are a vast and empty void stretching beyond the distant horizons and there are few identifiable landmarks. When a place was found that provided abundant food, it had to be marked so it could be located again. Such a place was the area of Kovik Bay. Here the waters teemed with arctic char centuries before the discoveries of Columbus, and during the spring and autumn months, the surrounding hills rumbled with the sound of the migrating caribou.

Here, facing the sea, the Inuit of long ago erected the Inuksook to mark this spot as a place valued for its fishing and hunting and a source of food. Here, these "symbols of man" remain today.

Flying northward from Timmins, Ontario, our twin engine Otter hugged the eastern shoreline of Hudson Bay. The last of the trees were fare behind us now – south of Great Whale River. To the west, the waters of Hudson Bay stretched beyond our vision, and to the north and east, there was nothing but a boundless land of tundra, rock, rivers and lakes.

INUKSOOK

Below us, flowing to the sea, was the Kogaluk (Big River), where we had experienced a fabulous fishing adventure the year before. Another half hour of flying brought us over the Inuit village of Povungnituk with its sand landing strip, but to our surprise, we continued on our northbound flight.

"I thought we would be taking a float plane from here up to the Kovik River," I said to the pilot.

"The Eskimos have a strip up there now," he returned.

"Oh, how is it?" I asked.

"Don't know. I've never been in there."

Another 250 miles finally brought us to Kovik Bay. On the shoreline, near the river's mouth, four beached freighter canoes pointed to a half dozen tents, and on top of a high ridge, behind the camp was the shortest landing strip I had ever seen. The tundra had been cleared and marked along each side with rocks wrapped in bright orange plastic. Another strip of the bright material was flapping in the wind at the end of a broken canoe paddle braced upright in the large pile of rocks that had been cleared to make the runway. Beside it, was a group of grinning men, women and children waving their greetings as we approached.

After bouncing to a "white-knuckled" landing on the spongy tundra, the Inuit helped us unload our gear and carry it down to the tents. Promising to pick us up "in a week or so", the pilot waddled the Otter back along the soft strip and lifted off, heading on a southbound azimuth, and home.

The Inuit here were from Ivujivik (Place of Broken Ice), a village about fifty miles farther north where Hudson Strait joins Hudson Bay. Their whole livelihood depended upon their skills at hunting and fishing, and Kovik Bay was a favorite area, just as it was for their ancestors of centuries long past.

We had come here to catch arctic char, and in our tent as we hurriedly rigged up our tackle to get in a couple hours on this first evening, I asked Peter Auduluk, the head man at the camp, if the fish were plentiful in the Kovik.

"No problem," he grinned. "Lots of char in river. Big char! You see. Kovik best place for char."

His predictions proved to be correct. My initial cast in a pool just below a stretch of white water, a short way upstream from our tent, resulted in a vicious strike followed by an arm-tiring conflict that finally came to an end in Peter's landing net. Holding up a large char by the gill cover, he flashed his biggest grin yet.

"You see? Peter tell you. Nice char. You happy now?"

Happy I was indeed, for our first few hours on the Kovik was even more gratifying than we had expected. My fishing buddy and I must have caught and released over a dozen char ranging from 10 to 15 pounds.

The char is a salmon that is found in the cold, arctic waters all across the roof of the world. Wherever it is encountered, anglers seem to agree that it is one of the most tenacious fighters of all the game fishes. It is an anadromous fish, moving out into the saltwater just after ice out, then back up the freshwater rivers to spawn in mid-August.

We were on the Kovik in early September. Before the end of the month the arctic weather would begin to deteriorate. Between "ice-out" and "ice-in" – early July to mid-September – there are but a few weeks suitable for sport fishing.

Peaking in August, this short period is a blend of all four seasons. Snow and ice from the precious winter may still be found in the shade of rocky outcroppings while the combined spring and summer finds the tundra ablaze with a tantrum of tiny flowers and mosses of unbelievable color. The autumn was evidenced by the early gatherings of caribou and waterfowl preparing for their annual southward migrations.

While we were here, the char were constantly on the move up and down the rivers. Where large numbers were found one day, there would be few, if any, the next. However, the fish were not difficult to locate. We caught them in the eddies beside stretches of roaring rapids, or near the mouths of feeder streams, or in the channels between islands and the main shoreline. Once contact was made, the action was always fast and furious.

The char also makes for an excellent dinner fare. It is delicious fried, broiled, baked or smoked. In the Inuit tradition, on a couple of occasions, we even ate it raw. Immediately after being taken from the river, and cold as ice, the firm, pinkish-white meat was surprisingly quite good.

Fresh from the sea, the char were healthy and strong, and at this time of year, they were mostly silver with blue-green backs and a scattering of pink spots along their sides. It is when they are land-locked or have been in the freshwater for quite some time that the male fish take on their colors of brilliant oranges and reds that are somewhat of kin to the arctic sunsets.

Our average char would probably weigh about 10 to 12 pounds, but regardless of their size, the Inuit always called them, "Ikalupik" (Big Fish).

One afternoon, in a side pocket below a long, heavy flow of undulating water, I fought and landed my largest char of our trip. We estimated it to be just under 20 pounds, and it was taken on an ultra-light spinning rig. Far off the record it may have been, but it was my thirty-fourth fish of the day – all over 15 pounds. I put down my rod and leaned on the gunwale of the big freighter canoe.

INUKSOOK

"I've had it!" I told my fishing buddy. "I've caught all of the char I care to for this day."

"Must be getting' old," he muttered.

As he continued to catch and release one fish after another, I was content taking pictures and pondering on how minute and insignificant I felt surrounded by the endless boundaries of this barren wilderness.

"What is it about this far north country?" I wondered. "What are the mysterious forces and unknown powers that seem to cloud the rational and logical thoughts of man, prodding his desire to return again and again to the Arctic?"

Perhaps the answer lies somewhere out there in the endless reaches of emptiness that make up this land beyond the trees. Maybe it is the unique and simple form of beauty found on the tundra or in the silence and loneliness that forever exists in the Great Barrens.

It may be its nearness to the magnetic polar attraction that deviates one's thinking as it does the action of the compass needle. Possibly, it may even be so deemed that man should never know the answer, and there should always be some things that are unreachable to him in this world of wonders.

Looking at my big char in the bottom of our canoe, I realized how typical this species is of all that is the Arctic. Like the Inuit, it is exceptionally strong and of great endurance. Like the aurora, it radiates with the hues of iridescent colors, and in keeping with the wide extremities of this land, the char's habitat covers most of the Arctic regions across the roof of the world.

Stories of arctic adventures, and especially those of char fishing, are always intriguing, but only a relatively few anglers undertake the journey to this faraway land where these gallant fish are found. There are those who travel from Chicago to try for tarpon and snook in the Florida Keys, and some will junket from New England to fly-fish the blue ribbon trout waters of the West, but the Arctic always seems to be so extremely remote and so very distant. And, it is, but this fact only lends to the fascination and romance of such an unforgettable experience.

I have pursued the arctic char from Alaska to several rivers along the coastline of the Northwest Territories and from the streams feeding Hudson Bay to the rushing waters flowing into the fjords of Baffin Island. Each adventure stands on its own merits, and it would be difficult to single out any one of them as being the most memorable.

Wherever the char are found, they are a challenge, but aside from that, a venture to the Arctic is more than just the sensational fishing. The overwhelming emotions that plague an individual when he is a part of this immense, lonely and isolated void are truly staggering. And, the occasion to live in day-to-day contact with the Inuit, whose culture is still in its transition from the very primitive to the modern, only increases one's wonder and admiration for them.

Combining all of these things – the fishing, the land and the people – one is not only pressed with the desire to return repeatedly to the Arctic, but he also acquires the makings for a lifetime of fireside memories.

Ever since my very first journey to this remarkable land, I have become so captivated by everything about it that I am addicted for life. Now, regardless of the distance and difficulties involved, I must somehow, someday return once more. The Inuit and the Inuksook will be there to welcome me back, I'm sure.

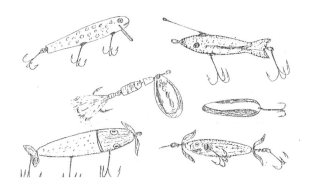

HOW SOME FISHING LURES CAME TO BE

I'm not a fishing lure collector as the term would imply, but I've certainly accumulated more than just a few over the years. Who wouldn't have, after a life of being involved in almost every facet of the piscatorial sport?

From the time I was a barefoot, bib overalled bluegiller, armed with a willow pole and a Prince Albert Tobacco can of red worms, to my present status of being a seedy old graybeard who has fished all the way from the tropics of Central America to the Arctic barrens beyond the tree line, I was there doing it all.

For over half a century, I've been actively engaged in fishing tackle retailing and wholesaling while, at the same time, expounding on the subject via radio, television and the written word of the outdoor publications. So, in light of all this, it seems only natural that I should have amassed a whole passel of lures along the way.

Most are the product of ideas created by tackle companies through their research and development departments. However, some have come to be strictly by accident, or often through nothing more than just plain, dumb luck.

Being a writer, these stories have fascinated me as much, if not more, than actually seeing how many different lures I could collect.

Take that simple metallic fish bait know as a "spoon", for example. Somewhere around the year 1820, it is said, a guy by the name of Julio Buel was eating his lunch while seated at the end of a boat dock. Accidentally, while stirring his coffee, he dropped his sugar spoon in the lake. As he watched it wobbling toward the bottom, a northern pike, the size of his leg, inhaled it and disappeared.

WALLAH! Ed Eppinger's famous, fish-getting' Dardevles, along with several tons of other metal variations, were the result.

Another interesting story came from a small village in Finland where a serious shortage of bait fish prodded commercial fisherman, Logie Rapala, into finding another way of coming up with enough salmon to feed his family and his neighbors.

HOW SOME FISHING LURES CAME TO BE

Pondering on the problem, Rapala came up with the idea, "If you can't take 'em with the real thing, why not fake it?", or in the Finnish words to that effect.

Anyway, that's when he carved a couple of small fish replicas from a hunk of pine, stuck fish skins on the sides, along with a hook or two. He then wrapped a line around each hand and trolled his make-shift shads far out behind his boat. His pulling on the oars, as he rowed the boat, gave the lures just enough of an erratic movement to stir the hunger pangs of one salmon after another.

It just so happened, a pair of traveling American fishermen witnessed the event, and to shorten the tale a tad, Ray Ostrum and Ron Weber set the Rapala family up in the lure manufacturing business, while they, in turn, promoted the new product around the globe.

"RAPALA" lures have since become a legend, and the reaction they spawned was unbelievable. At first, due to slow production, the supply was far too short to meet demands, and as the media spread stories of amazing catches being made, the response was immediate and in riot inciting proportions.

Fishermen in the United States went berserk bidding crazy prices for the scarce Rapalas. Clerks in tackle shops were offered bribes by customers to save lures for them from incoming shipments. One salesman even reported being threatened when suspected of hoarding the amazing fish catchers just to drive prices up.

A few enterprising dealers, with extremely limited inventories, even began renting a lure for $25 a day with a $15 refund being made when it was returned. So few returns were made their supplies of rentals disappeared before a week was out.

The final outcome of the "Rapala Rush" revolutionized prices throughout the whole fishing tackle industry. When it was suddenly realized that sport fishermen would pay almost anything for something they really wanted, the retail price for all other lures jumped from the average of about a dollar to three or more times that amount across the board.

Eventually, as supplies increased, things did level off a bit, but by then the virus had already spread to all fishing tackle items. Prices would never return to the pre-Rapala days.

On an entirely different occasion, I remember having a personal hand in the birth of another lure. As far as I know, this one never made it big in the sales market, however. While the idea worked, it was too easily "home made" to be profitable for mass production.

It all took place when six of us went on our first lake trout expedition to Ontario. It was in the early spring, not long after "ice out", and we had been told, "The trout will be up at that time of year."

HOW SOME FISHING LURES CAME TO BE

Being from largemouth bass country in the lower Midwest, we mistakenly took that to mean, "Bring plenty of surface lures," which we did. Actually, it meant the trout would be on the reefs and not down in the deep holes as they are in the summer.

Our surface lures were useless. What we should have been armed with were Dardevles. The few we had caught trout all right – lots of 'em – but the spoons quickly became casualties, that first morning due to being snagged on the reefs and a couple of big line breaking pike that ran off with them.

In the cabin that evening, my friend "The Judge", pilfered split rings, treble hooks and pieces of wire from other lures. With two of us helping, he attached them to an old beer can opener. The next day, the "Manatou Can-do", as His Honor christened it, captured several nice lake trout, a couple of huge pike and one out-of-season muskie.

I also vividly recall yet another story of how a new fishing lure came to be. It took place several decades ago at the National Fishing Tackle Manufactures Show in Chicago. Jim Lough, a long time friend of mine, had just been named Vice President and Sales Manager of the old South Bend Tackle Company.

When the show closed, at the end of that first long day, we were both ready for a change of pace. So, after a couple of hours attending various company cocktail parties, we taxied to one of Chicago's finer steak houses for a late dinner. It seemed everyone in the tackle industry had the same idea, and the parties at the hotel were continued in the restaurant's bar and lounge while waiting another hour for our table.

Anyway, to shorten a story still a bit on the foggy side, we finally made it to bed somewhere between 2 a.m. and an hour before the show opened at 9:00 the next morning.

My night was the shortest in history, and not being in the mood for anything in the way of a solid breakfast, I headed for the hotel's coffee shop.

The place was packed with all the tables and booths filled. However, the familiar figure of Jim Lough waved me to an open stool beside him at the service counter. Neither of us was quite up to par. In fact, Jim allowed as to how he felt like he was just before crossing over "the last great portage", so he asked the waitress for the Bromo Seltzer dispenser on the back bar.

Now that dispenser was mounted on a metal stand with a small sign on the top. It was made of grooved plastic, so if you tilted it to one side, the message read, "FOR HEADACHES", but tilting it the other way caused it to read, "FOR COLDS".

As we sat there talking about the new items we had seen at the Tackle

HOW SOME FISHING LURES CAME TO BE

Show, Jim kept playing with the dispenser, tilting it back and forth again and again. Suddenly he stopped, and with raised eyebrows, and we looked at each other.

"Maybe you should hang a hook on it, Jim," I suggested.

He did, and the lure became known as the "South Bend Optic".

When it was introduced the following spring, we gave it a try and found it to be a walleye killer. It went over great at first, but like so many other "flash-in-the-pan" lures, it faded away to become another memory in someone's lure collection.

Considering all of the many variations in both mass produced and hand crafted fishing lures already in existence, plus those being created each year, it's doubtful lure collectors will ever run out of new and different pieces to add to those they have already accumulated.

However, if their interests should begin to wane, delving into the background to find out how some of those odd-ball lures came to be, their stories may offer a new and even more challenge quest.

Anyway, it worked for me and some of the tales I have found may even be worth a book on the subject some day.

*   *   *

HOW SOME FISHING LURES CAME TO BE

The previous story first appeared in its original form in the September/October 2002 Issue of *"HUNTING & FISHING COLLECTIBLES MAGAZINE"*.

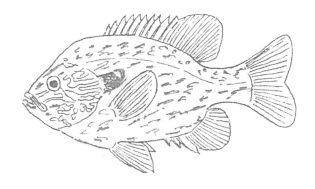

COUSIN REDEAR

Be they kith or kin, some visitors who overstay their welcome fast become a pain in the neck. . . and possibly other parts of the anatomy as well.

'Tain't always so, however, as was the case several decades back, when a rebel cousin from the deep south migrated north of the Mason-Dixon Line to take up permanent residence in the pits and ponds of the central Midwest.

To us, he is known as the "redear", a country cousin of our bluegill. Back in the land of cotton and mint juleps, where he originally hailed from, this spunky little member of the sunfish family goes by several aliases such as, "yellow bream", "shellcracker" and "stumpknocker".

Perhaps one reason he has been so warmly received by us is due to the fact he is less prolific than his

COUSIN REDEAR

Yankee relative, and less likely to overpopulate a lake with stunted fish. Then too, he tends to be a tad larger than the average bluegill. In fact, in his down home waters Cousin Redear will, on some occasions, tip the scales as much as an unbelievable four pounds or more. Now, that would be some kind of critter to reckon with on ultra-light spinning and fly tackle.

Like our bluegill, "Cuz" is a friendly looking little fellow and you wouldn't think he would be much of a trouble maker at the end of a line, but then... There are a couple of old sayings, something about "deceiving looks" or "not judging a fish by his gill covers", or in words to that effect.

Now in most lakes, Cousin Redear is somewhat of a wanderer, at least more so than some of his sunfish family who tend to socialize with others of their kind. His preferred habitat is around stumps, roots, logs and submerged brush. This occasionally causes him to hang out in the same bailiwick with another one of America's most popular pan fish... the crappie.

It may also explain why he sometimes turns up on the same stringers or in the same live wells belonging to those dedicated brothers of the crappie chasing fraternity.

But gettin' back to his Yankee Cousin: Family traits of the two are shared equally in several ways. Their markings may vary a bit, but their body shapes are similar. And when it comes to flavor at the dinner table there is no identifiable difference. They are both deee-licious!

It's those reddish-orange tips on the ear flaps of the gentleman from the south that makes him so easy to recognize. In clear water, even at the end of a long leader, his brilliant ears stand out like the lights of a new church on a dark night in Alabama.

While the two clans show mutual physical features, the redear does boast of a few variations besides his colorful ears. He is seldom a top-water feeder like his Yankee cousin with the solid blue epaulets. This little rebel prefers to hang out near the bottom, as he pigs out on tiny mollusks and crustaceans rather than insects near the surface.

Small snails are among Cousin Redear's favorite foods, and he is quite capable of crunching the shells with a series of stout teeth-like grinders located in his throat. Hence his other moniker, "shellcracker". Also, like most of the sunfish family, he will not hesitate to appease his appetite with a diet of worms and tiny minnows if they are available.

My first encounter with "Ol' Cuz" took place when I was a small boy. One summer day, with our gang of barefoot, bib overalled urchins, we decided to try our luck fishin' a farm pond on my Grandma Jenuine's lower acreage. Toting willow poles rigged with kite string, corncob floats and rusty hooks, plus our Prince Albert Tobacco cans loaded with red worms, we scooted under the barbed wire enclosed pasture, side-stepping fresh cow chips all the way.

By noon, the five of us had each landed a few small bluegills. One of mine was quite a scrapper and a little larger than the others. But, it was different in another way too. It looked a lot like a bluegill, except its ears were edged in bright orange. Anyway, it was added to the meager mess we cleaned for our shore lunch.

After we beheaded, gutted and scaled them, the little carcasses were embedded in balls of clay from the pond's muddy bank. Then we placed them in the burning embers of our shore lunch fire where they were baked until the mud balls were solid. When broken open, the steaming white meat inside was savored with both delight and pride.

Following our banquet, we baited up again, struck our willow poles in the mud bank and laid back in the sweet smelling clover as we watched our corncob floats and speculated as to what future paths we would follow when we got to be big boys.

The final outcome of this youthful adventure resulted in my being introduced to Cousin Redear and a lifetime love affair with the piscatorial sport.

Today, my angling methods as well as my fishing equipment have changed for the better. Ultra-light spinning rigs and 4 weight fly rods armed with artificial lures and feathered hooks are now my favorite way of tackling the job. There are times, however, while using an ultra-light spinning rod, and no matter how delicately they are presented my offerings of spinners, jigs and weighted streamer flies are ignored.

That is when the ways of my boyhood surface once more and I find that adding a grub, worm, cricket or some such morsel to the hook of my artificial enticements seems to sweeten them just enough to make a dull day's activity immediately brighter.

Frankly, though, I prefer to even the odds a tad when doing battle with "Johnny Reb" and his "Blue Belly" cousin, and at the same time make angling for them a bit more of a challenge.

In keeping with the traditional way of settling matters of honor, as it was in the days of Rhett Butler and the Old South, my duel with the bluegill and the neon-eared guy from the plantation ponds can be elevated to an even higher level.

It's easily done by simply using barbless hooks or by mashing down the fangs on the lures already in use. 'Tis a far more honorable and sporting way to go about it, don't you think?

Beside, it makes removing a hook from a small mouth a heck of a lot easier. And, having no barb on the hook makes little or no difference in the number of fish caught or lost.

While cane-poling and spin-fishing are more often preferred by some, my personal yen is toward the fly rod. Since the redear's dwelling is usually around the stumps and brush piles near the bottom, as is the crappie's habit, using the long rod does present another problem.

Fast sinking fly lines or long, weighted leaders should be used. Also, since tiny shrimp and mollusks top the list on Cuz's favorite menu, a well stocked fly box featuring a selection of 10 and 12 sized nymphs in various patterns and dark colors are a must. And, I always remember to back them up with an old favorite - a brown muddler.

Many years of close contact with Cousin Redear have left me with a single unconquered quest.

One of these days, I've just plain gotta get my carpetbaggin' keester down to the land of General Lee so I can tie into one of those humongous, four pound stumpknockin', shellcrackin' Redears... Or, is it "Red Years", as a long departed fishing buddy of mine used to call 'em.

ONCE UPON A BAR STOOL

It was smack dab in the middle of "the long wait", the between seasons for anything important, that is. Deer, ducks and geese were out. Turkeys were yet to come in. And the lakes were too thin to walk on the too thick to throw a lure into.

With a cup of steaming coffee in hand, I stepped out the door to check on the weather so I could plan my day. It was windy, raw and rainy with a bit of snow mixed in.

"DAMN! Should not have looked," I disgustedly muttered, returning to the house. For want of something better to do I spent my day cleaning guns and sorting fishing tackle that had twice already been cleaned and sorted. Late in the afternoon, I slouched down in an easy chair with a book I'd been wanting to read, but somewhere in the first chapter, I must have closed by eyes.

"Conking-out," Pet calls it.

"Meditating," says I. Whichever, the book fell from my hand about the same time the phone rang, or maybe it was the other way around. Anyway, the annoyingly cheerful voice invading my ear-ball belonged to Mort Swango, a long-time hunting and fishing buddy.

"Hey, Jack, what ya up to?"

"Meditating," I muttered.

"Huh! Doesn't sound all that important. Anyway, June tells me she's going to some kind of a gal's whatever this evening with Pet and Betty, so why don't ya come over here? We'll putts around in the rec-room for a while, have a tiddley or two and burn something on the grill.

"The Judge said he'd join us, but he may be a bit late."

By the time I arrived, Mort had a batch of martinis chilling in a pitcher and a fly-tying kit all set up on the bar top.

"Pull up a stool," he said as he dropped an olive in my glass. "June gave me this fly-tying kit for Christmas a couple of years ago, and I never got around to using it. Thought maybe we'd feather up a few hooks for the spring bluegill. You ever do any tying?"

"Once, a long time ago. It was a disaster."

"Well, while I was waitin' for you, I got to thumbin' through this old copy of Field & Stream I found in the basement, and I came across this recipe for tying a thing called an 'Irresistible'. The name kinda sold me, so I got to thinkin' maybe the bluegills would go for it too, come spring.

"What size hooks you planning on using, 10s or 12s?" I asked.

"I only have 10s and 14s, so why not use 'em both? And, oh yes, I have some light tan deer hair for the bodies, and this mallard hen plumage will work for the hackle. Only thing I didn't have was somethin' red for the butt.

"I think every fly should have some red on it someplace, so I scrounged around and found this dyed chicken feather. It came from a Japanese-made Indian war bonnet I wore to a Halloween party a few years ago.

"By the way, how's your drink?"

"Hit me."

As he was swirling the ice in the pitcher, a knock was followed by the sound of a door opening.

"Hey, Judge, you finally made it!" said Mort. "How'd you like a martini?"

"The only time I ever said 'No' was when they asked me if I'd had enough," said His Honor. "What have you two no-accounts been up to?"

"Fixin' to tie up a few Irresistibles for catchin' bluegill," I answered. "Where ya been?"

"Well, since late afternoon I've been listening to arguments in a divorce settlement. The two idiots couldn't agree on who was to get what in dividing the assets. Never heard such a squabble in all my life.

"They had already spent the past six months splitting up everything and were finally down to the last three items. That's where they were hung up and neither would budge an inch."

"What were they fussin' about?" asked Mort.

"Oh, they were hagglin' over a cut glass wine decanter, an original painting by that guy, Dali, and an old flintlock rifle that had hung over their fireplace.

"She was demanding all three. He was willing to divide 'em up, gambling on the flip of a coin to see who got first choice. But, she'd have no part of it."

By now, Mort and I were so wrapped up in the Judge's story, we recessed the fly-tying and listened as we sipped our libations.

"How'd it all come out?" I asked.

"Well, I ruled in favor of the husband. I thought he'd already been more than fair with her since she got the house, the furniture, the car and two bank accounts.

"I believe I made the correct decision, too, and I was glad he won the flip."

"What'd he finally end up with?" asked Mort.

"Why, something he could use, of course – the old muzzle loader and the wine decanter. After all, who would want a bunch of melting clock faces lookin' down on you from the wall?"

"Best I make a fresh batch of martinis," sighed Mort.

By the time we got around to tying the Irresistibles, we were having trouble focusing in on the number 10 hooks and the tiny number 14s were impossible. After several attempts, we finally got some deer hair wrapped on a shank. Then came the hard part. The mallard plumage and the feathers from the war bonnet just plain didn't want to cooperate.

We were all fingers and thumbs as the three of us tried getting into the act at the same time, while arguing as to how it should be done.

"Must be our advancing years," said Mort. "They say sight and hearing are the first things to go."

"That's also debatable," countered The Judge.

Eventually, we proudly admired our first Irresistible. Once we got the hang of it, each succeeding fly took less time to tie than the one before. They were supposed to be dry flies, but when The Judge test hopped one by placing it gently on the surface of his martini, it went straight to the bottom.

"Oh well, wet flies are best for early spring anyway," said Mort. "Maybe we can get together next week an' whip up some dries for later in the season."

A little past 8:30 we were admiring eight of the little rascals perching on the bar top. Not even one came close to resembling any of the others.

"Hey, I don't know 'bout you guys, but I'm getting' hungry enough to eat a road-killed skunk," I said. "Don't ya think it's time we raided your pantry, Mort?"

My suggestion met with unanimous approval, but just before we could retire to the kitchen, our wives walked into the rec-room.

"Hi, ya pretty, little ol' hunk of lovin', you," I blurted out when I saw Pet.

"Hi, yourself, you old goat," she returned, leering at me with a look of suspicion.

"What have you fellows been up to, asked Betty, "as if it isn't obvious?"

"Been tyin' Earie-ziss-ta-burples," slurred Mort.

"From the looks of things, I'd say 'Irresponsibles' would be a better word for it," said June, eyeing the spent olive picks in the ashtray.

Anyway, with the arrival of spring, Mort, The Judge and I headed to our favorite strip pit with fly rods in hand. To our amazement, our "Irresponsibles" rewarded us with catches we couldn't believe. The bluegills actually chewed them up.

There was only one hitch, however, and we couldn't quite figure it out. No matter how hard we tried, we were never able to tie matching replacements that worked half as well as those originals.

Maybe it was because we ran out of feathers from that Japanese-made war bonnet and had to use red ibis plumage instead.

THE FLOWER OF FISHES

One late winter evening at BJ's Rod & Gun Club the between seasons doldrums were at their peak and the subjects of our yarn-spinning sessions had already reached the rerun stages, producing boring yawns from the listeners.

Somehow in the retelling, the spread of antlers on that storied buck someone missed had grown by several inches, the distance at which that one-shot kill we had heard about so many times had lengthened another fifty yards and the sizes and weights of the fish some of the members had been bragging about for years were now getting close to record book proportions.

There were also noticeable gaps of silence when even the more talkative of the regular patrons drifted into quiet trances as they stared aimlessly into the swizzled pools of their libations.

THE FLOWER OF FISHES

As I remember, it was Big Ernie's elbow jabbing me in the ribs that snapped me back to the present.

"Hey, Jack. I know you and Da Judge have catched about every kinda fish dat swims. Which kind do yous like fishin' for da most?"

I turned to The Judge but all I saw were raised eyebrows, shrugged shoulders and open palms gesturing that the honor of answering Big Ernie's question was all mine. A glance down the bar revealed a row of faces turned my way waiting to hear what I had to say.

"Well, Ernie, that's a tough one to answer off hand. When you try comparing the different species there are too many variables. The largemouth bass, bluegill and crappie we find right in our own backyard would have to be close to the top of the list because they are so readily available to us.

"Then too, the saltwater varieties are in a class of their own. The tarpon, for instance, has got to be the most spectacular jumper of all and the power of a big snook hitting your lure will jar your eyeteeth.

"But I've also like fly-rodding for trout out in some of our western streams and it's hard to beat smallmouth bass and big northern pike up in Ontario. Of course, there's no way I can leave out the arctic char. It's a hell of a fighter and one of my very favorites, and. . . Oh, yes, I almost forgot 'the flower of fishes'."

THE FLOWER OF FISHES

"DA WHAT?" Ernie's forceful question demanded an immediate response.

"That's what Saint Ambrose called the grayling," I said.

"What's with dis grayling thing, an' who's dis Ambrose guy?" asked Ernie.

"Saint Ambrose was the Bishop of Milan back in the fourth century. I guess he was somewhat of a nature lover and a fisherman.

"As for the grayling, for years I had looked at photos and art sketches and had read bits and pieces about that fish, but I was never in areas where I could catch one until I made my first trip to the Northwest Territories."

"I'll buy you annudder one of dem bourbons and branches if ya tell us 'bout it," promised Ernie.

"Best offer I've had today," I said, sliding my empty glass down the bar to where BJ was already mixing a new one for me. In my mind, images were already forming of my first adventures with grayling.

My fishing buddy, "Catfish" Jack Ennis, and I were trolling for lake trout our first morning at Great Bear Lake. We had boated and released several nice ones and about noon we beached our boat for a shore-lunch. While our guide, Bill, was firing up the Coleman stove, I picked up my ultra-light spinning rig and strolled over to where a little stream flowed into the lake from somewhere out in the tundra. About fifty yards up stream, I waded out to a gravel bar and flipped a tiny, pink mini-jig into the deeper current along the far bank.

Darned if I didn't get a strike on that first cast. It was a small lake trout, weighing only a couple of pounds, and I held it up for Bill's approval.

"Good," he acknowledged, waving a skillet. "Now get another one like that and we'll have our lunch."

My next cast completed our menu and like we always say about shore-lunches, it was the best we had ever tasted. When we finished eating, Ennis stretched out on the soft tundra to have himself a siesta, so I returned to the stream with my ultra-light to play a little, "Catch 'em...let 'em go".

"I've taken a half-dozen trout on as many casts," I yelled over to Ennis a short while later. "Should I press my luck and go for another?"

"Go for it," he grumbled, rolling over on his side. "Whata ya got to lose?"

I moved a few yards farther upstream to where my cast could reach across to a larger pool. In that gin-clear arctic water I could clearly see the pink hackle on my jig pulsating as I slowly worked it along.

From somewhere deep among the rocks a ghostly, slate-colored apparition formed. It rose slowly at first. Then, suddenly flashed in an all-out charge, snatching my jig and streaking for the bottom. The abrupt bowing of my little spinning rod triggered

THE FLOWER OF FISHES

involuntary reflexes that jerked barb into bone and detoured the dash for freedom in an upward direction.

In the center of a spreading circle, the stream's surface parted as my phantom came clearly into view displaying itself in a graceful arching leap settling my question of, "What in the hell is that?" The answer: A beautiful arctic grayling – my very first.

Now, at long last, one of these gallant little fighters was cavorting about with my line slicing up the pool's surface. As I worked the fish closer I could easily understand why anglers in centuries past referred to it as "the standard bearer". In comparison to its relatively small body, its dorsal fin was massive. When it darted past my hippers, that fin was waving through the water with all the pride of the flag atop the dome of an Indiana court house. A couple of more sweeping sprints and my unyielding prize finally came to the net. It scaled out an even three pounds and was truly a magnificent little creature.

On the male grayling, that sail-like appendage is a bit larger and more shapely than on the female, but on either, it is far more outstanding than the dorsal on any of its freshwater cousins. The fish's coloration is a tad difficult to describe – kinda like painting a mental picture of the constantly changing hues of the northern lights.

THE FLOWER OF FISHES

Depending on how the sun's rays strike it, the body is basically a bluish-gray, but with an iridescent sheen of pinkish-bronze. Its sides are marked with a scattering of tiny black dots and that imposing dorsal fin is highlighted with even rows of short, pink dashes. The pelvic veins are streaked with rose.

The grayling's mouth is small, with the maxillary not extending beyond the center of the eye. As for its overall size, the world record is a little over five pounds at the most.

The species is also encountered in extremely limited numbers in the mountains of Montana and Wyoming and in the High Uintas, but that far south, the few that are taken will seldom reach one pound in weight. It is a very fastidious little rascal with a definite preference to the coldest and purest of waters. It was once found in the state of Michigan. In fact, there is even a town and a military base named "Grayling" in the north-central part of that state.

Sadly, however, logging activities there years ago caused environmental changes that created thermal pollution of the waters. That was the undoing of this magnificent little fish in that area. Recently, efforts have been made to reintroduce the species there, but the results have so far failed, and that's really too bad. Now, we must go all the way to the Arctic and sub-Arctic regions to fish for them.

THE FLOWER OF FISHES

While my first grayling was taken on a pink mini-jig, we also took them on 16th ounce Dardevles, Rooster Tails and Mepps spinners. Mostly, we enjoyed fishing for them with a fly rod using a wide variety of flies and patterns.

Our best fishing came in late evening and early morning when schools of feeding grayling were sucking in their fill of some unknown insect hatch. The calm surface was dimpled as if a gentle rain were falling. That's when we witnessed the thrilling spectacle of those little fin-wavers clearing the water in a perfect arc as they came down on their selected morsels.

It's truly exciting to have one of them at the end of a light fly line tippet. One morning I was fishing with a small dry fly, hand tied and given to me by my friend, Doctor Conklin, before leaving home. It was nothing more than a brush pile of brown hackle with a scarlet tail. It bore no name other than the one I hung on it – "Conk's Classic".

Anyway, I landed and released several nice grayling on the "Conk", and after losing a couple, I examined the hook and discovered why. Doc is a fly fisherman of the old school and a believer in doing it the hard way. That fly he gave me was tied on a barbless hook.

The grayling is not only a creature of fascinating beauty, but its unique and delicate flavor at the table is a gourmet's delight.   In contrast to other fishes, it has a delectable quality all its own.   There is a hint of the herb thyme in its appealing taste which probably accounts for the name some of the science boys called it long ago – "Thymallus Arcticus".

"Well, Ernie, that's all I can tell you about the grayling," I said when I finished my story.

"Besides, The Judge and I are ready to eat dinner."

"Yeah, and I don't wanna keep ya, but what I wants to know is hows come those scientific guys can get us to da moon an' back, but dey don't know hows to clean up our lakes and rivers so's I can catch some of dem graylings around here?"

"That's something I've been asking myself for years, Ernie.   In fact, just the other day that question was brought home again when I came across an article relating to that very thing in an old outdoor magazine among my collection of antiques, so I cut it out."

Taking the folded clipping from my wallet, I read it aloud:

"Is it not worth the while of the American people to ponder this matter of clean water and matters of kindred significance?   The abuse will be stopped when the pubic wishes it stopped and not before.   Yet people have been writing and talking about this for a long time."

THE FLOWER OF FISHES

"That's a timely bit of editorializing, don't you think? I clipped it from an issue of the old <u>FOREST & STREAM MAGAZINE</u>, dateline: September, 1919."

"WILLIAM...HE GOOD CARVER TOO"

Few people have ever heard of Ivujivik. It's an Inuit (Eskimo) village on the northwest tip of Quebec's Ungava Peninsula where Hudson Strait joins Hudson Bay. Translated, Ivujivik means "place of broken ice."

William Nataraluk lives in Ivujivik. Fewer still have ever heard of him. That is more their misfortune than his.

Here, in the world's harshest environment, William's very survival depends on his skills as a hunter and a fisherman. His traps and nets capture the arctic fox and the arctic char. With harpoon and rifle, he pursues the beluga whale, the seal, the caribou and the great white bear.

So vast and barren is this Arctic world that it tends to lose itself in its own infinity. Always silent and nearly void of human life, its bewildering expanse dwarfs one's presence and self image.

While his lifestyle borders on the primitive, William is gifted with the unbelievable talents of a truly fine artist.

Inuit art in North America goes back thousands of years, probably having its beginnings long before the Inuit people migrated across the Bering Strait on what was once a land bridge connecting Siberia with Alaska. As with most ancient cultures, themes of their art forms were influenced by supernatural beliefs passed down by the elders and shamans from one generation to another.

Many of the artifacts were carved amulets and fetishes used to decorate their tools and weapons with the hope they would repel demons and appease good spirits, thus bringing success to their hunting and fishing. The explanation of their earlier works has long been lost in antiquity, forever remaining with the artisans of bygone ages who alone could provide meaningful answers. Such items are now museum pieces.

However, some of the Inuit art carvings of old, and to a greater extent those of more recent times, were not created so much for a spiritual expression, but rather as a simple pastime to relieve the hours of boredom dominating the long days of darkness during the arctic winters.

"WILLIAM...HE GOOD CARVER TOO"

While the subject matter of past works has changed from the grotesque devils and idols of sorcery to those of animals, birds, fishes and people common to everyday life, the medium used has remained essentially the same – mostly, serpentine and soapstone and the ivory tusks, bones and skins of the caribou, seal and walrus.

It was not until the past four or five decades that modern Inuit art has become widely appreciated and collected by connoisseurs throughout the world.

Since World War II, the widespread use of float plane travel has opened the remote areas of the arctic to hunters and fishermen who have been venturing to the far north in ever increasing numbers. Naturally, many of these sportsmen have become fascinated with the uniqueness of the land and its people and also with their art creations.

Today, Inuit cooperatives in some of the larger arctic villages are shipping their carvings to a host of art galleries and gift shops in southern Canada and northern United States. For the Inuit, this has been a means of supplementing meager incomes and attaining independence from government welfare bureaucracy.

Sadly, however, the growing popularity of the finer art has led to a flood of counterfeit replicas which are of mediocre quality at best.

In an attempt to cash in on the excellent works of highly recognized carvers, the number of "wanna-be" artisans has increased dramatically. So too, did slip-shod duplication of popular subjects, and near assembly line production in some Inuit Co-Ops has replaced originality and creativity.

Better selections and finer quality pieces may be found at specialized dealers and galleries, but many of the choice carvings are acquired by visiting sportsmen directly from an Inuit carver in his own environment while enjoying some of the world's best fishing as a bonus.

This is how I have obtained many of the pieces in my own collection, and they mean so much more to me than some of the carvings purchased from dealers in Canada and Alaska.

It has been said that anyone who travels to the Arctic and spends some time with the Inuit, returns with the urge to write a book about it. I believe there is more truth than fiction in that statement. For on each of my seven ventures to this unbelievable land beyond the trees, I have been deeply touched by every aspect of it. And the experiences have added to the value of my collection.

I first met William Nataraluk at an Inuit tent camp on the Kovik River, some fifty miles south of Ivujivik. He spoke very little English. His friend, Peter Auduluk, introduced us. He spoke a bit more.

"WILLIAM...HE GOOD CARVER TOO"

"This William," said Peter. "He know many fish in river. You catch big char. You see. William, he take you."

Then, as an afterthought, Peter added, "William...He good carver, too."

Although he didn't realize it, Peter's introduction answered two questions I was about to ask. First, the char fishing was evidently very good. Then, also, there was a possibility of adding a piece or two of Inuit soapstone or ivory sculptures to the collection I had acquired from my precious arctic visits.

William acknowledged our introduction with a nod and a snaggle-toothed grin and gestured for me to get in his 20 foot freighter canoe.

Its interior was a mess. Most Inuit boats usually are. The grease, blood and spent cartridge cases sloshing around the wooden ribs in an inch of oily water bore visual evidence to yesterday's seal hunt.

I picked up a small piece of a mandible with a couple of teeth still attached. William grinned as I examined it.

"Oogruk (seal)," he said

A few miles upriver he cut the outboard and I flipped a small, orange Dardevle lure into the eddies below a rapid. It immediately triggered an arm-tiring standoff that eventually terminated when William netted and released an arctic char of maybe fifteen pounds.

"WILLIAM...HE GOOD CARVER TOO"

Two more casts produced two more fish of equal size. Apparently the river was full of them, so I handed my back-up spinning rig to William, motioning for him to use it. Soon we were each fighting a char at the same time.

"Iklupik (big fish)," grinned William as he held up the two char for me to photograph.

Later, on the way back to camp, I gave him that extra rod and reel as a gift. For a moment his eyes sparkled. Then his smile faded to a frown and he handed it back, shaking his head. However, I insisted he was to keep it, and after reconsidering, his sober face brightened again and he nodded.

The Inuit are a proud and resourceful people. They detest the Canadian Government's welfare program and they hesitate accepting gifts without reciprocating in some manner.

"With gifts, you make slaves, like with whips you make sled dogs," an older man once explained the culture behind it.

That evening, William came to my tent and presented me with one of his soapstone carvings. It was the likeness of an otter with an arctic char in its mouth.

Peter Auduluk was right. William was indeed an exceptionally good carver. His gift settled the debt he felt he owed me. We were now even.

My collection of Inuit carvings has been acquired from various places on previous visits to the arctic: Coppermine, Povungnituk, Fort Chimo on Frobershire Bay, Pangnertung on Baffin Island and Alaska. They are all typical examples of Inuit art, but this sculpture by William Nataraluk is truly outstanding.

Its flowing lines breathed life and motion into the stone, and the work ranked with some of the finest pieces I have ever seen. His subjects are inspired by the mammals, birds, fishes and people he knows best from his encounters in everyday life.

While returns from the sale of his works are gratifying, he carves because he likes to, and he continually strives to produce new and better sculptures.

I do not pretend do be a connoisseur of any art forms. I only know what I like, and for me, the creations of William Nataraluk are prized collectibles. Peter Auduluk was right.

"William...He good carver, too."

DESTINED TO MEET

Once upon an August morning in Canada's Northwest Territories, a brace of lake trout were spawning on a rocky reef in Great Bear Lake. One of the small eggs drifted down into a crevice between two boulders where it was safe from the ravages of predators that often invaded the nesting areas.

In a few months, the fertilized egg became a fingerling lake trout. Staying close to the protection of his rocky home, the tiny fish would occasionally dart out to feed on minute aquatic insects.

About the same time these events were taking place on the Arctic Circle, several thousand miles to the southeast in Indiana, a newborn baby boy was blinking his eyes, trying to focus in on the strange new world surrounding him.

Almost half a century later, the fish and boy were to meet in a huge bay in the northeast corner of Great Bear Lake. By now, the little fingerling had become an awesome creature of some fifty pounds and as many inches in length. The boy, too, had matured, and now as a man, he had ventured to this far North Country to fish its arctic waters.

From the very first day of my arrival, I was completely captivated by the unique beauty and bewildering vastness of this treeless land. Exposed here is some of the earth's oldest rock, the Precambrian Shield. Pushed upward when molten hot, it was to cool and form the igneous crust covering the core of magma deep within the planet. Down through the eons, the shield has withstood the eroding elements. Even the great glaciers that ground and gouged and cracked it could not destroy it.

Today, these immense outcroppings make up the islands and shorelines of one of the world's largest freshwater lakes. With over 12,000 square miles of surface area, Great Bear drops off to depths of more than four hundred feet. Its waters are so clear the wobbling flash of a Dardevle spoon can be seen fifty feet below. Looking down into these untainted depths, boulders the size of houses are visible trailing off into still deeper chasms.

Such bottom structure affords plenty of natural cover for fish of all sizes, but in such gin-clear waters they tend to spook easily. Trolling along the drop-offs with heavy spoons at the end of long lines produces the best results.

"Hi, my name is Bill, and I'm to be your guide during stay here," said the young Canadian who welcomed me as I stepped to the dock from a float equipped Norseman airplane.

"Hello, Bill. I'm Jack. How's the fishin'?"

"Oh, I believe I can put you over some mighty fine lake trout. The catching is up to you," returned Bill with a grin.

Bill had spoken the truth. By the end of my first fishing day at Great Bear, I quit counting the number of lake trout I had taken and released. They averaged from 8 to 10 pounds in weight.

Because these frigid waters are free of ice only eight to ten weeks of the year, the growth rate of fish is extremely slow, and my best fish on this day was about 15 pounds. It was a male, in its spawning colors of reddish-brown with the leading edges of its pelvic and anal fins marked in snow white.

The next morning Bill ran our boat 30 miles to the far side of McTavish Arm where the Arctic Circle slices through the upper part of Great Bear. The fishing here was even better. We estimated most of the trout would range from 12 to 18 pounds.

In the early afternoon we beached our boat near a place where a small river meandered from the tundra-covered hills to wed with the waters of the lake. It was an ideal spot for a shore lunch.

"See if you can catch a couple of eating size trout from the river," said Bill as he was building a driftwood fire.

I picked up my ultra-light spinning rod and flipped a tiny orange Dardevle in the stream. Two casts were rewarded with a pair of "bookend" trout that were perfect for our menu.

After our meal we doused the fire, cleaned up the site and spent an hour doing a little exploratory fishing upstream. We caught and released several beautiful arctic grayling with our ultra-lights. The sun was warm and pleasant and it felt good to stretch our legs and be out of our rain suits for a while.

Although there had not been a cloud in the sky all morning, the breeze blowing across the arctic lake waters felt as though it was coming directly off the polar ice pack farther to the north. So, whenever we were out on the lake, we wore our rain suits. They made good wind breakers and kept our body heat from dissipating.

DESTINED TO MEET

Following our break on shore, Bill
and I were back at our catch and
release game, trolling our flashing
spoons along the edge of the drop-offs.
We kept it up until late afternoon, but
Bill wanted to try a few more places
before leaving for our two hour run
back to camp. As we moved slowly
along, he was standing in the stern,
steering the boat with the raised
tiller arm of the outboard motor.

"We've been doing OK trolling, but
I'd like to get you into a large
concentration of trout so you can cast
for them," he explained. Our boat
glided past a point and into the mouth
of a huge bay. It was quite deep, but
we could clearly see at least thirty
feet down to the rocky bottom.

"There's a trout," pointed Bill,
"and there's another... and another...
and there's one! This is what I've
been looking for."

With a long, looping cast, I lobbed
a large, yellow and red Dardevle toward
the rear of the bay and began a slow
retrieve.

Thirty feet below the surface, the
big trout was lying in the shaded
protection formed by an overhanging
boulder. Sly, suspicious and hesitant,
his long years of experience had keenly
honed the survival instincts that had
allowed him to exist well beyond the
average life span of his species.
However, on this particular day, the
flashing of something passing within a

few inches of his lair seemed to be too much of an easy prey.

As he moved forward, his great mouth opened, the sucking surge of the intake engulfed the spoon.

After almost half a century, destiny had finally brought this giant fish of Great Bear Lake and the man from Indiana together. Now, the two were joined at the opposite ends of a nylon line. The artificial lure had worked its deception, and this was as it should be. For the intelligence of man is just a cut above that of the fishes – at times, that is.

The anti-reverse was set on my casting reel when the crank jerked backward to a sudden stop. My rod bent so far down the second and third guides were beneath the surface. There was no slashing strike, no telltale jerking, just a strong, steady pressure that increased with intensity as the reel's drag slipped and the line moved out toward the mouth of the bay.

"I'm onto a fish," I yelled, "and I think he's a good one!"

Bill cut the throttle and tilted the outboard up on the transom. A huge bulge boiled the water about a dozen yards from the boat as the big trout came to the surface and then plowed even deeper as it headed for open water.

"Play 'em easy," Bill shouted. "He IS a good one! What size line are you using?"

"Seventeen."

"Play 'em easy!"

"The drag is working perfectly," I said as the fish stripped off more line in its bid for freedom.

"Just don't force 'em. Play 'em easy," insisted Bill.

By now, the trout had moved farther out into the open waters of the big lake. Then it turned in a wide, sweeping arc and the boat drifted around with it. Slowly, little by little, I was able to recover some line. The pressure was heavy and steady, but the distance between the fish and the boat gradually closed.

As Bill stood holding a long-handled boat net and looking down into the water, he kept repeating his coaching demands of, "Easy...easy."

Finally, the big trout moved slowly up from the deep and closer to the boat. That's when Bill went for him, leaning far over the side with his arm deep in the water. His scooping motion met the heavy fish head-on, but as he tried to lift it, the net's long aluminum handle was bending almost to the breaking point.

I held my rod in one hand and grabbed the hoop with the other to keep it from snapping off. Bill tucked the handle under his armpit and locked his fingers in the net. Together, we hauled the fifty pound plus giant over the side.

"Holy cow!" panted Bill. "It's the biggest fish I've ever had in my boat."

DESTINED TO MEET

When all of our hoopla and back slapping died down, Bill fired up the outboard and we headed back to camp.

"I don't know about you, but I'm about to starve to death," he shouted above the noise of the motor.

"Yeah, and a dram or two of the 'creature' might be in order, too," I yelled, "...just to celebrate, you know."

Our return trip across the open water that night was a wondrous experience in its own right. The calm, perfectly mirrored surface of the lake was marred only by the wake spreading out behind our boat and the midnight sun reflecting in the water, painted its glories across the arctic sky. It was a scene we would always remember.

The big lake trout in this story now graces a wall in the National Freshwater Fishing Hall of Fame at Hayward, Wisconsin, where thousands of visitors can enjoy seeing it each year.

Who knows? Perhaps even now, another fingerling trout is swimming in the arctic waters of Great Bear. And maybe, when he becomes a giant laker he, too, will be destined to meet up with a man who is but a mere babe today.

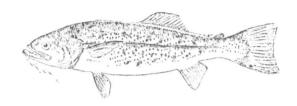

WHERE THE CHAR ARE

"Something is wrong... It's my nose... Why is it so cold?" I opened one eye and immediately closed it. "Why is the tent so bright?

"The tent? What tent? Where am I?"

The gray matter suddenly faded... My body jerked and I sat upright, fully awake, and with everything in clear focus.

No wonder my nose was cold. Our camp was on Baffin Island at the north end of the Kingnait Fjord where the Tongait River Valley leads into Auyuittuq (The land that never melts.)

Yesterday, following our departure from the Inuit (Eskimo) village of Pangnirtung in twenty foot freighter canoes, we worried our way through fifty hairy miles, dodging the ice bergs in Cumberland Sound, to arrive here late last evening.

WHERE THE CHAR ARE

The August sun was stalled just above the horizon when we crawled into our sleeping bags at midnight. Now, at 4 a.m., it was shining brightly, high overhead.

"Brrr!" I scrambled into my clothes, breathing clouds of icy vapors as I did. Pete and Lloyd were still sleeping as was the rest of the camp. So, picking up my fly rod, I stepped from our tent into a most awesome and unbelievable world. It surely must have been this way, unchanged, since the beginning of time.

Never have I felt so alone, so small, so insignificant. Walled in on both sides by high snow-capped mountains, the tops of which were lost in ice-chilled fog banks, I stood in frozen wonder, looking north up the broad and seemingly endless valley of the Tongait. Here, disappearing into the distant horizon, was a vast and lonely void of nothing but tundra and giant boulders, worn smooth by the grinding of ancient glaciers.

In the distance, its source hidden somewhere up on a cloud-shrouded peak, a silver ribbon of a cataract dropped thousands of feet down the mountain side. In the perfect stillness I could faintly hear the cascading water, but hiking to it would surely cover five to ten miles. I decided against it.

Behind me, from out in the fjord, the tide was moving in pushing the fresh water of the river back up the valley. I waded, ankle-deep, to where

114

WHERE THE CHAR ARE

I could fish the pools on the far side of a gravel bar. The char that took my gaudy, salmon egg colored streamer fly were all small but scrappy critters.

Engrossed in catching and releasing them, I failed to notice the gravel bar was now almost completely submerged. I became aware of the rapidly rising river only when it began lapping around the top of my hip boots. I was forced to scramble to high ground. This was my first experience fishing in waters where the tides ran as high as thirty feet.

By the time I hiked back to camp, breakfast was ready. Pete and Lloyd were up and had arranged for one of our Inuit guides to take us out into the fjord where the char were much larger than those in the river. The winds were light, the water calm and the incoming tide had brought with it several icebergs from Cumberland Sound to add a bit of drama to the already captivating panorama.

Most of our fish were taken where the mountain sides dropped straight away into the dark, cold water of the fjord. Near its mouth where it widened, however, the shoreline was lower and more accessible. There, we beached our canoe and waded along the shoreline, casting out to the drop-off.

It was here I tied into a char as ornery as any I have found on all my trips to the Arctic. It hit my tiny, orange spoon with such a jolt I almost lost my grip on the rod. The crank of my spinning reel whirled backwards, the knob beating my knuckles, before I could get it under control to let the drag take over.

Stripping off yards of line, the char headed toward the large ice floes a couple of miles to the south in Cumberland Sound. For a while, I believed he would make it, too, but for some unknown reason he made a sudden hundred and eighty degree turn, and I was cranking frantically trying to pick up the slack. I was in water above my knees, my legs spread for stability, and that fish charged straight for me, actually running between my boots. I have never had that happen before or since.

I thought the char was lost for sure as he turned in a wide arc behind me and streaked for deeper water. The line pulled around the back of my right hip boot. All I could do was thrust the rod tip down in the water while hopping around on my left leg as I tried to kick my right up and over the tightening strand of monofilament. On the third attempt, I made it but took a quart or two of water over the top of my left boot in doing so.

Finally, I was able to work the now spent char in on its side where I could get a couple of fingers under its gill covers. Estimating it to be at least fifteen pounds, I removed the hook and set it free. Then I waded ashore, collapsing on the rocks for a much needed breather before emptying my hippers of the icy water. Of all the fish I've taken over the years, this is the one I will always remember.

Pete had been watching the fiasco from a distance and he wandered over to air his thoughts.

"The Moscow Ballet may think your pirouettes are great," he said, "but personally, your fishing techniques are lousy."

One evening after we had returned home, Pete and I were sharing our experiences with some of our friends at BJ's Rod & Gun Club.

"Ya know, there's one thing I don't understand," said Luke. "I enjoy my trips as much as you guys, and I like going to different places an' catchin' different fish. Why, I've caught just about every kind there is, with the exception of this char you talk so much about.

"So, what I'd like to know is why you spend all your effort, time and money making repeated trips to the Arctic for this one particular species when you have so many other places and other fish out there just waiting for you?"

"Well, Luke", I said, "what you're saying makes a lot of sense, but it's difficult to explain. It's another world up there in the Arctic, and the char, well...

"Years ago, I caught my first char up in the Northwest Territories, where the Coppermine River flows into the Beaufort Sea. Later, there were trips to Quebec's Ungava Peninsula, to the Kogaluk River, near Povungnituk and to the Kovik, near Ivugivik. Now, we have this new and fabulous place to add to our log of adventures.

"While BJ was charging our glasses with one last round before dinner I was giving your questions some serious pondering. My thoughts returned to Baffin Island, to the Kingnait Fjord, and to the overwhelming scenery of Auyuittiq. I pictured once more the boundless reached of the barren lands that make up the Arctic, and I remembered the enchantment of our day-to-day living in close contact with those amazing people – the Inuit.

"I thought about the roaring rivers and the treeless hills and I recalled a cold night on the tundra, watching the most fascinating display of the aurora I have ever seen. I could almost feel the chill from those icebergs in Cumberland Sound. And, perhaps more than anything else, I could feel again the power of an arctic char, fighting my rod until my arm ached.

"All of these things only take place where the char are.

"So, Luke, in answer to your question, 'Why the Arctic?' and 'Why the char?', the only thing I have to say is: 'Why not?'"

PART II

OF HUNTS AND HUNTERS

"I come to the forest, to be a part of the wild, and if I should return with an empty game bag, my day is still a success."

Riley McKay

THE SWAMP

Some looked upon it as a couple hundred acres of valueless wasteland. Others loudly proclaimed the neglected eyesore to be downright shameful and that something should have been done about it years ago. Several even referred to it as the rectum of creation. Then there were those who allowed as to how, if it were drained and cleared, it just might produce a fair-to-middlin' crop.

For a few of us, however, it was one beautiful hunk of real-estate. We simply knew it as, "The Swamp", and as far as we were concerned, it was the site of some of the best damned duck hunting in the surrounding countryside.

To the migrating flights of waterfowl, it must have looked like an island refuge smack dab in the middle of paradise. For this timber-ringed sanctuary was surrounded by seas of corn and soybeans stretching as far as the eye could see.

Physical access to The Swamp was a drudgery in itself. Hoofing it two miles down a long abandoned, deeply rutted and washed out country road to the property line was the only way in. Then it was a fight through a tangled jungle of briars, twisted willows and rotting dead-fall to reach the water's edge.

From there it was all splash and stumble through a quagmire of mud and decayed vegetation only to end up against a wall of head high cattails. Beyond these lay the open water.

The deepest spot in the whole slough would be hard-pressed to reach three feet, and beneath that was another foot of the most stinking, blue-black muck one could imagine. Wading through it was always a cotton-spitting task that threatened a coronary and was usually accompanied by a string of four letter adjectives that would shame a Marine drill instructor.

Originally, The Swamp was constructed in the mid 1800's as a reservoir for the now long defunct Wabash and Erie Canal. Over the years it had changed ownership several times, and now no one was quite sure who held the title.

Its survival was credited to the fact that the neighboring landowners just plain couldn't agree on how to dispose of the rotten apple. However, a stroke of luck finally solved the dilemma and preserved The Swamp in its natural state.

It came about one day while the debate among the farmers was still dragging on. Two devoted duck hunters, "The Judge" and his attorney friend, "Double L" were jump-shooting woodies along a drainage ditch when they blundered onto The Swamp.

Shooting hours were almost over and they were short cutting their way back to where their jeep was parked. As they were passing the edge of a heavily wooded thicket, they heard the din of quacking ducks reverberating from deep within the tangled jungle. The sound was just too much for the two died-in-the-wool ducksters to pass up without investigating.

Somehow, in the fading twilight, they fought their way through the nearly impenetrable growth to where they could see the open water. There they found the surface literally covered with babbling mallards cramming their corn-filled gullets with a salad of swamp water smart weed.

Now, since both hunters were involved in the legal profession and had business at the county courthouse early the next morning, they paid a visit to the Assessor's Office to check the plat record books. They thought if they could find out who owned this duck hunter's dreamland, perhaps they could lease it during waterfowl seasons.

THE SWAMP

As it happened, their efforts paid off far better than they could have possibly believed. They discovered what the bickering corn growers had not taken time to consider.

It seemed The Swamp's legal owner had long ago abandoned the property and had completely disappeared. The place was now listed on the county records as being up for a delinquent tax sale. The assessed evaluation was next to nil, and the two duck hunting legal-beagles lost little time in completing the necessary papers that made them bona fide owners of The Swamp.

The windfall prompted an urgent meeting of our gang who hunted and fished together. Under Double L's leadership, immediate plans of action were assigned priorities. Signs were posted along the perimeters of the property - "NO TRESSPASSING - NO HUNTING - VIOLATORS WILL BE PROSECUTED".

There were only a few hunting days left in the current duck season and an assessment must be made to estimate the work needed prior to next fall's opening day.

So, The Judge and Double L decided to make an exploratory hunting expedition to The Swamp. For this, they borrowed my old Marine Corps inflatable boat. It had three air chambers - bow, stern and floor. Made of a tough rubberized material, it was light weight and like a leaf on the water. But, lacking a keel, it was difficult to control and was a tad skitterish to say the least.

Arriving at The Swamp, they pumped up the craft at the edge of the cattails and paddled out to set their decoys.

"If we're going to get any shootin' today, we'd best camouflage this tub some way," said The Judge from his seat in the rear of the raft.

"You're right," agreed Double L. "I'll take care of it."

Leaning far out over the bow, he grasped the leafy branch of a live willow and took a healthy swing at it with his little belt ax.

"NO! NO! DON'T!" yelled The Judge as Double L's movement scooted the unstable raft backward. But, his warning was lost in a "POOFFF" of escaping air when Double L's ax missed the tree limb and found a home in the boat's forward air chamber.

"OH, WOW! WHAT ARE WE GOING TO DO NOW?" gasped Double L as the bow collapsed leaving him standing deep in the muck with the water lapping over the top of his hip boots.

"I'll tell you what WE are going to do," ruled His Honor with a tone of authority. "WE are going to sit up here in this end where it's halfway dry while the REST OF US tow what's left of this scow out of this mess. That's what WE are going to do!"

Double L sheepishly handed The Judge his shotgun, and with the bow rope over his shoulder, began floundering through the glue-like muck. Panting and cussing, he fell flat several times before reaching dry ground. Needless to say, plans for construction of permanent duck blinds received an immediate boost to the top of the priority list of work to be done before the next waterfowl season.

In the months that followed, permanent frameworks were set in place at three strategic locations in The Swamp. The backbreaking work was accomplished in the heat of a dry summer. And, the weekend prior to opening day of the new hunting season was spent camouflaging the new blinds.

At last all was ready and the long awaited day arrived with just one little problem – the weather. It was not only bluebird clear, it was downright hot.

At daylight, Double L was in his personally designed blind accompanied by The Judge. A dozen or so mallards departed as they were setting out their decoys, but other than a blue heron and several flights of blackbirds, nothing else was observed flying all morning long.

Following a brown bag lunch, they spent the afternoon as they had their morning – slapping mosquitoes and searching the cloudless sky, which also remained duckless.

Along about four-thirty, in the middle of Double L's longwinded dissertation of preferred shot sizes

THE SWAMP

for water-fowling, he suddenly stopped and reached for his shotgun.

A lone mallard hen was winging her way over the east end of The Swamp. Both hunters began blearing away on their duck calls. The amateurish bellowing of their garbled highballs should have sent her streaking for the next county, but for some unexplained reason, the hen turned, heading toward the decoys.

"Let me take it from here," whispered Double L, hunkering lower in the blind.

"We're in your blind, so she's all yours," said The Judge.

Now, it must be said, when he settled down, Double L did a masterful job of calling. His long-range "come-hithers" turned the hen each time she changed course, and his low, feeding chuckles drew her closer and lower on each pass.

"Next time around, I'm gonna take 'er," he breathed, letting his call dangle from its lanyard and flipping off the safety of his 12 gauge.

The duck banked high over the ash woods and headed for the open water. Locking her wings, she commenced her long glide to the decoys. That's when a single shot sounded from just inside the timber across from the blind. It didn't even come close.

With a loud, "Quaaack", the duck shifted into high gear and skee-dattled, leaving a fuming Double L standing in the blind with a red face and gaping mouth.

"Who in the world...? HEY, WHOEVER YOU ARE, GET TO HELL OUT OF HERE. THIS IS PRIVATE PROPERTY," he shouted.

From out of the woods and into the water waded a brown clad figure carrying a shotgun. With a wave of his hand, he waded directly toward the blind. It was Double L's Uncle Charlie, one of the most notorious game-hogs and poachers in the county. It seems he had recently heard of his nephew's vested interest in The Swamp and had invited himself to hunt this opening day of the new duck season.

"Is that you, Double L?" he called, stumbling forward through the water and muck.

"KE-BOOM!" Double L's Remington sent a shot-string high over Uncle Charlie's head. It was immediately followed by the clatter of another round being shucked into the chamber.

"DON'T YOU 'DOUBLE L' ME YOU GOOD-FOR-NOTHING S.O.B.! GET YOUR POACHING ASS OUT OF HERE AND STAY OUT!"

Any and all respect for family ties disappeared with that single shot on the first and only duck of the season's opening day.

All things being considered, that grand opening fiasco was not at all typical of the many fine days that followed during our first year of hunting at The Swamp. Limits were logged time and again. Each hunt was an adventure in itself and worthy of

THE SWAMP

being recalled at future yarn-spinning sessions.

There was, however, one other memorable moment when things didn't go quite as planned.

We all gathered with our wives one evening to celebrate the close of the first hunting season at The Swamp. The event was a formal duck banquet hosted by one of our buddies and his wife at their newly redecorated home. A right fancy affair it was, too – coats and ties, party dresses and all.

Following cocktails and hors d'oeuvres, we strolled to their attractive dining room to admire a spread that would shame the finest of restaurants. The table was set with fine china and crystal and featured a large silver tray graced with eight beautifully roasted and garnished wild mallard ducks.

Being the self-appointed leader of our hunting fraternity, Double L stood at the head of the table. Heads were bowed as one of the wives gave the invocation, after which Double L announced, "I shall now carve the ducks."

Pushing up his sleeves and with fork in hand, he made a stab at the nearest duck on the platter. What happened next all took place within a matter of a few terrorizing seconds.

Double L's aim was a tad off center and that gleaming silver tray was a bit on the slippery side. When the fork's tine grazed his targeted bird,

129

that mallard plowed into the rest of the nesting flight, and they all took off like their tail curls had been dusted by both barrels of full-choked sixes.

The flight scattered in all directions. One duck plowed into a large chafing dish of giblet gravy which, in turn, did a double flip, spreading its contents around the dining room.

Walls, draperies, furniture, carpeting and assembled guests all received their share before the dish finally came to rest upside down in front of Mrs. Double L, who by now was staring daggers at her duck hunting spouse.

It's truly amazing how much surface area a single bowl of giblet gravy can cover. Needless to say, the dramatic incident officially closed our first year of hunting at The Swamp.

In the years that followed, "The Great Duck Dinner Disaster" headed the index of an ever growing collection of hunting yarns to be long remembered and often repeated at various gatherings of The Swamp's "Brave & Benevolent Society of Water-fowlers".

A BOY'S FIRST GUN

Some of my fondest boyhood memories are of those days of growing up on Grandma Jenuine's farm in Vermillion County, Indiana. There were those wonderful springs when life was new and all fresh and green. Dad and I would wander the woodlands together searching for the elusive yellow morels.

And, there were those barefoot summers when we caught bluegill, crappie and the occasional bass from the old mill pond. I always fished with red worms I dug from Grandma's garden while Dad favored using minnows, or as he called them, "MINNIES", he had seined from the "CRICK."

Then, there was that very special autumn I will never forget. The red and gold of the maples and the bronze of hickories and pin oaks mingled their glories with the green pines on the

hillsides.   We   followed   the   brook
edging   the   wooded   pasture   as   we
gathered walnuts and persimmons.

Dad   was   carrying   his   new,   mail
order,   Stevens   "Crackshot"   rifle.   It
was a little .22 caliber single shot, a
falling   block,   lever   action   and   the
first real gun I had ever seen.   Rich
colors of case-hardening covered the
receiver   and   its   deeply   blued
steelbarrel sported a front sight blade
of German silver.   The highly polished
stock   displayed   the   warm   luster   of
hand-rubbed walnut.

The   glint   of   afternoon   sunlight
reflected in its slightly curved metal
butt plate, and I caught a whiff of the
sweet   smelling   banana   aroma   from   the
Hoppe's   Number   9   oil   protecting   the
rifle's metal.

Dad's   1929   catalog   from   the   old
Sutcliffe   Company   of   Louisville,
Kentucky, priced the "Crackshot" at six
dollars,   and   a   box   of   fifty,   .22
caliber   "Kleanbore"   shorts   was   only
fifteen cents.

Today,   such   prices   cannot   be
imagined, but they were a tidy sum back
in   those   impoverished   years   of   the
Great Depression. For those working on
the farms and in the coal mines of the
surrounding area, it would often take
several weeks of back breaking labor to
come up with enough savings to buy that
rifle and a box of cartridges.

"This will be yours some day," Dad
told me.   I promised your mother I
would   keep   it   until   you're   a   little

older, but I guess you're not too young to learn how to shoot it."

Using the high creek bank for a backstop, Dad lined up several green hulled walnuts on an old stump. I flopped down on my overalled belly, and he taught me how to hold a steady aim and squeeze off a shot. By the time we were ready to head back to the farm house I was plinking those nuts off that stump with some regularity.

Dad and I continued to have our memorable walks together in the wooded hills near Grandma's farm. At times, he even let me carry the unloaded rifle. With a gentle, but a firm hand resting on my shoulder, he strictly instructed me as how I was to carry and safely handle the little Stevens and how to care for it.

I was so proud of Dad's trust in me and I eagerly awaited the adventure of going to the woods alone carrying that rifle. But some things don't always work out the way they were planned.

There came a new and different life in the city with schools and jobs and girls and then, a great war that took me far away. When I returned everything had changed. Grandma and the farm were gone, all too soon, so was Dad.

Somehow, the little "Crackshot" had also disappeared, but it was not forgotten. It spawned a lifetime interest in firearms and shooting that I enjoy even today. Now, I have my own shotguns for trap and skeet shooting and for hunting. There are also the accurized handguns that won medals for me at the Camp Perry National Pistol Championships. And there is a collection of antique firearms — flintlock and percussion pistols and rifles that were a part of history.

There is a certain romance in collecting old guns. I can run my fingers over the initials crudely cut in the walnut grip of an 1851 Colt percussion revolver, and I try to picture the man who carved the "H.L.K.", and I try to vision what kind of life he may have led. When I fondle a cased pair of flint dueling pistols, I wonder if they ever settled a question of honor and how it all came about.

Some of the guns from the Civil War era conjure up exciting mental pictures of flags waving as long lines of men in gray uniforms advance across an open field to where other men, in blue, wait behind stone walls and rail fences. I can almost hear the crashing of artillery, the high-pitched notes of bugles sounding the charge and the chorus of rebel yells.

Through all of this there still remained the haunting memory of my youth and that little Stevens "Crackshot."

Then one day there was a stranger at my door — a distant relative. He had a .22 rifle he believed may have belonged to my father and wondered it I would be interested in buying it.

A BOY'S FIRST GUN

I would, and I did.

It was like being reunited with a long lost friend, but the little "Crackshot" had seen some rough times since we were last together.

The colors of the case-hardening on the receiver had long since disappeared. There was little of the original bluing left on the barrel, and small patches of rust and pits showed here and there. Only traces of the finish remained on the walnut stock which was now deeply scratched and gouged in places.

The working action still functioned, but the silver front sight blade was missing. However a cloth patch, run through the dirty bore, produced surprising brightness and sharp rifling.

A visit to a friendly gunsmith did wonders for the restoration of my wounded rifle. A thorough cleaning helped more than anything. Some of the deeper dents and scratches in the stock were raised with steam, and there was a new, shiny replacement for the missing front sight. It was decided there would be no major refinishing, so it was to remain as near as possible to its original state.

Finally, the rifle was test fired on paper targets, and the fairly tight group in the black X-ring at twenty paces was most rewarding. Only then, at long last, was my little "Crackshot" brought home to rest on the wall of my den.

Now, one question remains: What will happen to it next?

My nostalgic feelings for this little .22 are not shared by my son. His interests lie with his own rifle – an Anshutz Match Model that has won many awards for him in competitive smallbore matches. So, what happens next? The decision must be mine, and mine alone.

Possibly, a scene from the past will be repeated. Perhaps there will even be long walks in the woodlands with my grandson. Could it be that a stern, but gentle, hand on his shoulder will steady his aim as Dad's did mine?

Maybe, just maybe, the little "Crackshot" will have another youthful admirer and it will once again receive the loving care and pride of ownership that only comes with a boy's first gun.

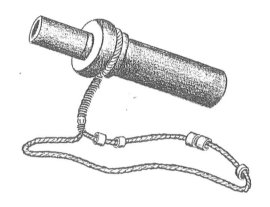

THE BAND

About the same time that Cricket was a clumsy, boot chewing pup growing up at a hunting club on the banks of the Illinois River, a small puff of down tumbled from a grass nest and into the water of a marsh in northern Saskatchewan. Now, under the watchful eyes of a protective hen, the duckling joined others of his brood exploring the world near his home.

By late July, the fledgling had grown in size and strength and had acquired the plumage of an adult mallard drake. The range of his wanderings had also expanded and there came a day when he experienced the most traumatic adventure of his young life.

Together with others of his kind, he was captured in a cannon net of a biological survey team from the U.S.

THE BAND

Fish & Wildlife Service. Working with their counterparts in Canada, they were on duck banding missions in the prairie wetlands of Manitoba, Saskatchewan and Alberta.

Over the years, millions of birds have been banded in North America. Many of these bands have been recovered and have provided vital information relating to migration, survival, life expectancy and other important facts pertaining to the study and management of various species of waterfowl.

When his turn came, our young mallard was taken from the net and held in the firm but gentle grasp of an apprentice wildlife biologist while his mentor crimped a loose-fitting aluminum band around the duck's right leg. The species, sex and estimated age of the bird were recorded in the field notes next to a number corresponding to that on the band. He was then released.

No longer was he just another anonymous duck. From now on he would be known as Number 1417-56374.

While these events were unfolding in Canada, far to the southeast, in a backwater slough along the Illinois River, Cricket, the young black Labrador retriever, was being trained for the coming hunting season. His schooling had begun with the playful throwing and fetching of sticks in the back yard, but now, it had advanced to a more true-to-life hunting situation. This included the sounding of a duck call, followed by the firing of a shotgun, and finally, the retrieving of a "dead duck dummy" thrown into a spread of decoys.

All things being considered, Cricket's education was progressing nicely by the latter part of the summer.

Up in Saskatchewan, the mid-September weather was beginning to deteriorate. Ducks that had been scattered in small family groupings were now gathering in larger concentrations. There was a restlessness among all waterfowl throughout the vast North Country. From the Northwest Territories, geese were winging their way southward in large "V" formations. Below, on the marsh waters, the ducks watched them passing high overhead, but they did not follow – yet.

Then, one day in October, with heavy, dark snow clouds on the northern horizon, thousands of birds lifted as one and the roar of their wing beats muffled the sound of the boreal winds. Wave after wave rose on the timing of some mysterious cue and headed out on a southbound azimuth. By the next morning, the Canadian prairies were void of ducks.

The huge flights funneled out of the provinces and crossed the border, pouring into the Dakotas as they followed the mighty Missouri River, the Souris and the James. Instinctively

they found the traditional migration
routes inherited from the millennia of
generations that had preceded them.

Some drifted into Minnesota and
Wisconsin where thousands of lakes
awaited them. They found the narrow
creek that would soon widen to become
the greatest of all our rivers. From
it the flyway would take its name –
"The Mississippi".

Here, in the "land of many waters",
they settled down to rest and to feed.
They would remain until the arctic
storms bore down upon them, freezing
the lakes and bringing deep snows that
would cover their food sources.

One bright autumn day, by the shore
of a shallow lake in the Horicon Marsh
Refuge near Fond du Lac, Wisconsin, a
well known wildlife artist photographed
a flight of mallards as they dropped
into a flooded planting of millet. One
bird in particular, the nearest drake,
stood out prominently in the foreground
of the camera's viewfinder. As he
approached, with his feet down for a
landing, the golden rays of the late
afternoon sunlight caught the glint of
a shiny metal band on the bird's right
leg.

A few weeks later, at his home
studio, the artist brushed the
finishing strokes on a beautiful
watercolor that was inspired by the
photograph taken that day at Horicon.
Some 1,500 signed and numbered prints
were made from that single painting,

and they were sold during the next few months at auctions held at <u>Ducks Unlimited</u> banquets across the country. Over a million dollars was raised from this single work of art. The money would go to aid in conserving the prairie wetlands of the North for waterfowl of future years.

By now, some 500 miles farther south, the autumn foliage had changed the countryside into a land of spectacular colors and beauty. Young Cricket watched, with cocked head and questioning brown eyes, as decoys were being repainted and fitted with new cords and anchors. Barking and prancing excitedly, he led the way down to the dock. His excitement was uncontrollable, and his momentum nearly carried him over the side when he leaped into the johnboat. As our boat sped through the shallow backwaters, Cricket whined with anticipation.

While smartweed camouflage was being added to cover the blind, he splashed around through the shallow water and muck as he explored the surrounding swamp. With humans and dogs alike, there was a pressing apprehension of the hunting season soon to come.

Finally, one cold November morning, along with two hunting buddies and the eleven month old Lab, we arrived at the slough in time to break out the thin layer of ice and distribute the decoys. When the task was completed, we sat in the blind sipping coffee from a steaming thermos.

Cricket crowded in close against my boot trembling with anxiety. I rubbed his ears while we were discussing the latest weather reports. Deep freezes and heavy snows had blanketed the upper Midwest states two days before, and prognostications were that the southbound front would soon be reaching our area.

Suddenly, Art pointed to the northern horizon, and his duck call sounded long range hailing notes. The Judge and I hunkered down in the blind and watched as a squadron of mallards swing in from on high. It was a large flight – fifteen or more birds. They cruised far overhead at first but turned to give our setup a second look.

The next pass was lower still, and as they locked their wings, a hen answered Art's feeding chuckle with a soft "quaaak". On the fourth go-around, several ducks dropped out of the flight. With wings cupped and landing gear down, they glided in over the decoys, pitching from side to side with necks craning for a better view.

Three shots sounded as one, followed in quick succession by two more. A trio of mallard drakes crashed into the icy water among the blocks. The last two discharges were wide of their marks, and the rest of the unscathed flight quickly winged high and away.

THE BAND

When the first shots sounded, Cricket bounded out through the shallow water, where he triumphantly pounced on the first fallen bird he came to. Art stepped from the blind, calling words of encouragement and praise, as he watched the dog's inexperienced retrieve.

The young Lab's return trip was slow. His mouthful of mallard was almost more than he could handle, and the awkward neophyte stumbled and waddled his way back. But he made it, dropping the duck at Art's feet and dousing him with a shake of a heave, wet coat before dashing back to bring in another bird.

Picking up the drake, Art was surprised to find a shiny metal band around the drake's right leg. The stamping read:

"1417-56374
ADVISE BIRD BAND - WRITE
WASHINGTON, D.C. USA"

That evening, relaxing with my boots off in front of a log fire, I studied the little aluminum band Art had given me, wondering what stories it could tell. A few weeks later, in answer to my letter reporting the kill, I received a card from the U.S. Fish & Wildlife Service. It confirmed that Mallard Drake Number 1417-56374 had been hatched in the spring of this same year. It further informed me that in August, the duck had been banded near Meota,, Saskatchewan, by a USFWS biologist from Columbia, Missouri, and that the band had been recovered in November, when the bird had been downed in the Illinois River bottoms near Beardstown.

In a way, I was disappointed and sad. I guess I was expecting more. Just what, I didn't know – perhaps something that would make the short life of Number 1417-56374 seem a little more meaningful.

I removed an antique duck call from where it hung by its lanyard on the wall of my den, and I slid this new band down along the cord to join others recovered from previous hunts. Examining the collection of tiny rings prompted my digging into a file cabinet to find the information cards relating to them. That's when I began to understand.

While the read-out on a single report card seemed more or less meaningless on its own, the collective data from several cards seemed to form patterns that could be of value to those who manage our wildfowl.

The life-span of the drake wearing this latest band may have been less than a year. But, one of the other reports revealed that a mallard hen was banded near Grantsburg, Wisconsin, more than two and a half years before the band was recovered on the Wabash River in Indiana. Another showed that a drake, banded at Big Sandy Wildlife Refuge in Tennessee, had made at least four round-trips up and down the flyway before a hunter retrieved the band near Stuttgart, Arkansas.

Perhaps the combining of such information would be important in formulating plans and regulations that, in turn, would be beneficial to the future of waterfowl. Perhaps even the scant life of Number 1417-56374 may have played some significant part in such research, and his short existence may have served a useful purpose after all.

I toyed with the little metal band once again and for some strange reason, I still felt that there was something missing. Could it be that there were even more contributions this young mallard may have made for his species? Something else that perhaps was not included here on his information card?

I guess I'll never know.

* * *

(This story first appeared in its original form in the April/May 1989 Issue of WATERFOWL MAGAZINE.)

"...IT'S A DAISY"

WHATEVER HAPPENED TO THE "VL"?

"When are you going to do something about this mess?" asks Pet.

"One of these days real soon," I promise, using the same words that have been getting me off the hook for months.

"Don't give me any more of that, 'one of these days' malarkey. I want this disaster cleaned up, and I mean NOW!" If it isn't, I'm going to..." Her voice trails off as she walks out of my den slamming the door behind her.

I hate den cleaning days, even though they only come around about every five or six months or when Pet gets mad enough to put the hammer on me. If there's one thing I've learned over the years, when her requests become threats, it's past time for me to at least go through the motions.

From the floor beside my desk, a

WHATEVER HAPPENED TO THE "VL"?

four year old pile of press releases
was given a new home in a trash bag to
be hauled to the dump. They were
joined by several dozen stacks of
culled out photographs from my files of
hunting and fishing trips to places I
can't even remember. Next, a stack of
road maps, fishing camp brochures and
old sporting goods catalogs half filled
the second bag.

In the corner, standing behind
several rod and gun cases, was an old
air rifle – a keepsake from my boyhood.
As I was wiping years of accumulated
dust from it, Pet barged in again.

"Just checking to see how you're...
What's that old thing?"

"It's a Daisy," I answered, fondly
rubbing the timeworn pine stock of my
treasured memento.

"Well, lah-dee-dah!!! I don't care
what kind of a flower you call it as
long as this catastrophe gets
straightened up," she declared, leaving
me alone once more.

"Humm... It's a Daisy," I mumbled,
repeating those words as they brought
back memories almost forgotten.

When I was a kid, it was the
aspiration of every American boy to
someday own a real-for-sure, genuine
Daisy BB gun. But, for most of us
growing up in the era of the Great
Depression, such dreamed of personal
assets were few and far between.

Our clothes were never more than
patched up hand-me-downs. If lucky, an
old Barlow pocket knife with one broken

blade, a baseball with a friction taped cover, a few chipped marbles and a couple rusty fish hooks were about all that made up a boy's prized possessions during those impoverished times.

Ownership of anything better was merely a figment of youthful dreams. Hours were spent studying the multitude of fabulous items in the "wish books" from Sears Roebuck and Montgomery Ward.

"Someday, when I get to be a big boy, I'm gonna have one of these," was the promise we made ourselves time and again. But, such fantasies seldom came true, although, one did for me on my twelfth Christmas.

How my bib overalled pals envied me when I proudly showed off my "brand-spankin'-new", genuine Daisy, Buzz Barton Special, BB gun. Dad had put in several extra hours working overtime and two years of convincing Mom before he came up with the $2.50 and her blessing to buy it for me.

"Every boy wants to have a Daisy of his very own someday," Dad argued, remembering bygone dreams from his own youth.

It wasn't that Mom was opposed to spending all that hard earned money for my Christmas gift as much as because of what happened just before my tenth birthday.

Duffy Patterson III is what happened. He was the first of our gang of barefoot urchins to own a genuine Daisy. And, it was his lousy marksmanship, one hot summer day, that

149

missed the cow on the label of a Pet Milk can and sent a ricocheting BB into my cheek within an inch of my left eye.

The sting itself wasn't what touched things off as much as it was the sight of a tiny speck of blood on my fingertip when I removed my hand from my face. With horrid expressions, Duffy and I stared at each other for a frozen second before I streaked for home screaming in terror.

"YOW! OH, YOW! MOM... MOM... I'M BLEEDIN' TO DEATH... DUFFY PATTERSON THE THIRD HAS SHOT AND MURDERED ME!!!"

Duffy, on the other hand, hightailed it in the opposite direction with visions of his own lifeless carcass swinging at the end of a lynch mob's rope beneath the rafters of the old covered bridge.

Actually, my own youthful demise came closer to reality when Mom grabbed me by the arm dragging me on a dead run down the dusty road to Doc Dunnwig's place. Doc had to treat us both for the "palpitations" before he could get around to examining my wound.

Cleaning the sweat and road dust from my face revealed the nearly spent BB had bounced off my cheek bone and was not embedded in my hide after all. In fact, the skin was barely broken. Nevertheless, my shrieking continued while Mom held me down so Doc could dab the minute puncture with iodine and cover it with a dime-sized patch.

The good doctor's fee for this professional service cost Mom a dozen eggs from her favorite layin' hen. In turn, it cost me the thumpin' of my life from Mom for being so stupid as to stand that close to a target when someone was shooting.

The whole fiasco resulted in two things taking place. First, Duffy Patterson III and I both became instant heroes in the eyes of our barefoot pals.

Duffy was now looked upon as being somewhat of kin to one of those famous gun fighters in the ten cent western magazines popular back in those days.

It was only after his father sentenced him to three days of house arrest, while listening to repeated lectures on safe shooting practices. Once it appeared his execution by hanging was not likely to take place, Duffy breathed a bit easier, and he began to revel in the glory of his newly won reputation. He played it to the hilt, too, even going so far as to carve a notch in the pine stock of his genuine Daisy.

I, on the other hand, ended up being the wounded survivor of the notorious "shoot-out", and I insisted on my patch of distinction after all trace of the tiny scab had completely disappeared.

The final outcome resulted in the delay of my owning a BB gun. It was only when Dad finally convinced Mom that I was now two years older and had learned a valuable lesson that she agreed to the purchase of my Christmas gift.

WHATEVER HAPPENED TO THE "VL"?

That's how I came by my first "genuine" Daisy, but it was not my last. Some thirty years later, when I was a "big boy", a representative of Daisy Manufacturing Company presented me with a Daisy "VL" rifle, so named for Jules Van Langenhoven, of Belgium who invented this new and unique shooting system.

Like many outdoor enthusiasts, I was fascinated with the "VL" from its beginning. It was an entirely new and different concept in firearms and not simply another BB gun of the type Daisy had been producing over the years.

Just think about it. Here was a REAL rifle, but without a firing pin, an extractor or an ejector. They were not needed because its ammunition had no primer, no powder and no brass casing. Yet, it would send a .22 caliber bullet to a target at a velocity of over 1,100 feet per second.

A round of ammo looked like a tiny cylinder of white chalk attached to the butt end of the same lead bullet found on a regular .22 short cartridge.

A single stroke of a lever under the gun's forearm compressed the air in a small chamber. When the trigger was pulled it released a jet of that air which, in turn, was heated by friction as it passed through a tiny venture opening. This detonated that cylinder of chalk-like propellant creating an expanding gas and driving the bullet through the rifled barrel. A sharp

152

crack was heard, just like an ordinary .22 when it left the muzzle.

The whole system was intriguing, to say the least. Even General Curtis LeMay, former Air Force Chief-of-Staff, referred to it as a "revolutionary development in the history of firearms."

The first Daisy "VL" and its most unusual ammunition were released to the public in 1966. Needless to say, its uniqueness created immediate interest in the shooting media and attracted interest in the military.

However, as swiftly and enthusiastically as it came into being, two years after the first rifles reached the market, the "VL", just as quickly, but quietly, passed into oblivion.

"What happened to the "VL"? I wondered as I stood there fondling my own rifle. "After all the hype it received in the beginning, what caused it to die so quickly on the vine?"

A couple of phone calls to gun dealers and distributors produced the same puzzling answer: "Daisy discontinued it."

"But why?" I asked. No one seemed to know.

It was all one big mystery that immediately fanned the fire of my imagination. As a writer prone to fantasizing and daydreaming, simply thinking about it conjured up all sorts of interesting mental scenarios and touched off a whole string of "what ifs".

"OH! WOW!" I gasped. "What if the "VL" was deliberately pulled off the market for reasons of national security? What if everyone involved in every aspect of its creation from the very beginning has been sworn to secrecy in an effort to hush up the whole thing?

What if our federal government, U.S. of A. and the Empire of the Pentagon thought the "VL" system was the greatest little ol' military asset to come down the pike since David invented the slingshot? What if, even now, the Daisy Company's research and development people are quietly working in a closely guarded limestone cave secluded somewhere in the Ozark hills as they make radical improvements on the "VL" that will belittle the secrecy of the Atom Bomb Project during World War II?

"What if the CIA, the FBI, the IRS and the Washington Post were, at this very moment, watching me, my wife, my den and my dog simply because I've been asking questions about what happened to the "VL"?

"Oh boy! What a story! I can almost see it in the tabloids now and under my byline, too. WOW!"

Reality, however, is seldom as exciting as daydreams. Contacting a Daisy company executive revealed the truth. The "VL" was caught up in a web of unforeseen circumstances.

WHATEVER HAPPENED TO THE "VL"?

Some 25,000 "VL" rifles were sold in its first full year of production. This wasn't bad considering it was something new and radically different. But then, along came the Federal Firearms Act of 1968 and its crippling effect on the entire firearms industry.

For Daisy it was a disaster. It made doing business with the "VL" virtually impossible. The development, production and marketing of such a new and novel shooting system were extremely expensive and required a tremendous amount of capital. It would take years to amortize these expenses before it could become cost efficient.

The new gun legislation wounded the sales and profits of many conventional firearms companies, but the initial development costs of their products had been written off years ago. For Daisy, however, with its new "VL" struggling for recognition and acceptance, it was different. There was no way they could economically buck the competition of an already existing market.

Today, the "VL" rests in the dusty museums of antique guns. But, unlike the flintlocks and percussion models of old, I can't help but believe that this rebel child of a new generation is but sleeping – biding its time while waiting to be resurrected someday in the future.

For those of us lucky enough to own a "VL" and a few rounds of its rare ammunition, it becomes more than a mere collector's piece. For us, it is a nostalgic connection with our lost youth, and that little bit of a kid in us will always look upon it as our very own, "real-for-sure", genuine Daisy.

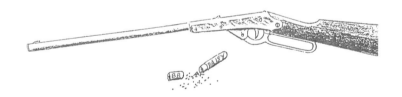

THE GUN CLUB

There are gun clubs, and then, there are gun clubs. First, there are those that are the epitome of excellence in every way – beautiful lodges at choice locations and private rooms with original oils of 19th century waterfowling. It's coats at dinner, and there is lace, and crystal and silver. And, it's always, "Mister" and "Sir".

In the end there is usually some truly fine gunning, where you can step from a boat into a comfortable, heated blind without so much as getting your boots wet.

I have enjoyed being invited to hunt at such a place on rare occasions (very rare), and I have found that it is rather nice to be pampered once in a while, but... well...

THE GUN CLUB

Then, there is that other kind of gun club, and personally, if I had my druthers, I will opt for it every time. Fortunately, I have had the opportunity to spend a weekend of hunting at such a club annually, and I have collected a wealth of nostalgic memories in doing so with some real down-to-earth people.

Arriving at the Gun Club (my kind of gun club) is almost like a homecoming. There are the coarse barks of tail wagging dogs I haven't seen in a year, and there are the back slappings and jovial greetings from the club members and pushers (a pusher is an antiquated term for a duck hunting guide) whose friendships I have come to value after sharing so many hunts together. And then, there is something else – something difficult to explain.

It's in the air. Perhaps it's the musty, but clean, smell of the river and the bottom land willows with their dried mud watermarks from last spring's flooding. Whatever it is, it's a welcomed difference.

The old two story frame house sits back from the river on eight foot pilings with a long, wide ramp leading up to the front porch. Even the raised level of the building is not enough to prevent the annual flood waters from creeping a foot or so up the wall of the main floor. Each spring the furnishings are lugged up to the second deck and then back down when the river recedes.

THE GUN CLUB

Over the entrance is a weathered plank with the faded painting of a flying mallard drake. The front porch is sort of a "ready room" where inverted hippers hang in rows along the wall and there are benches and boot jacks for pulling them off. There are hooks for insulated coats and rain gear and a bulletin board posted with the week's score sheet along with an ever changing assortment of cartoons featuring ducks, dogs and hunters. There is also a refrigerator, well stocked with after-the-hunt libations.

Other than the kitchen, the main floor has a huge room for dining and lounging. In front of a large stone fireplace, where flames lick at river bottom oak and locust logs, is a semi-circle of easy chairs. Here, you can slip suspenders from tired shoulders and put socked feet up as you enjoy a "sip of the creature" while reliving the day's hunt and solving the world's problems or, it you prefer, just forgetting them.

A couple of old wooden decoys, carved years ago by some Illinois "river rat", nest on the mantel. Above them hangs a framed print from a Ducks Unlimited auction. On the opposite wall is an aerial photo map of the club grounds with the various blinds pin-pointed. And, there's a long rack from where hand rubbed stocks and blued barreled shotguns emit the pleasant banana aroma of Hoppe's Number 9.

THE GUN CLUB

A typical day during the club's hunting season begins in that distant somewhere in the clouded webs of half slumber. The muffled drone of a pre-dawn outboard sputters to a stop and is replaced by the soft lap of after-wake against the river bank. There follows a short stretch of deep breathing quiet, soon to be reaped by the slamming of a downstairs door and the swishing tramp of turned down hip boots on a creaking staircase.

I roll over on my side turning my face to the wall with the hope that Ted, the club's manager, will go away. But, the snap of a light switch floods the bunkroom with an unwelcomed brightness.

"I can't believe you bastards drove all the way over here from Indiana just to sleep." It's 4 a.m. and Ted's bull voiced wake-ups are always such a memorable experience.

Stretches and groans and a muted blasphemy directed at a misplaced sock are interspersed with hoarse throated comments that would normally bring laughter, but wasted on the stupor of sleepy minds, they fail to spark a smile.

Toothbrushes and splashings of cold water gradually revive life and spirits, and the usual bantering includes loud demands heaped upon a die-hard sack hound to "Hit the deck, 'cause it's daylight in the swamp".

Soon, a half dozen suspender-backed hunters are sock-footing it downstairs

160

to breakfast and the planning of the day's activities.

WOW! That coffee has a real muscle this morning."

"What did you expect? No coffee is worth a damn unless you can float a horseshoe nail in it."

While a hardy meal is being consumed, drawings are held for the hunting areas. Intriguing names identify the blinds: "Bouillion Swale", "The Firing Line", "Big Island" and "The Point". Thermos bottles are filled with steaming brew, guns are slipped into cases and extra shells are jammed into hidden pockets. Down at the boat landing, while an excited Labrador barks and prances about, a pusher tunes up his duck call as he waits for the hunters.

The pushers are an intrinsic part of the Gun Club. They lend it their valued services and their unique character. They are river people, born and raised in towns along the Illinois – Pekin, Havana, Beardstown, Meredosia and Grafton. Educated to the river and its mysteries as much as anyone can be, they know its hazards and its pleasures. They know the fish and wildlife of its bottom lands, and more importantly, they know its waterfowl.

For most of the year the pushers work at various occupations. Some are boatmen, piloting the long tows of heavy barges laden with tons of grain, coal and steal. Up and down the Illinois, they guide the giant barge trains from Chicago through the hundreds of miles of channel bends, sandbars and islands to its confluence with the Mississippi above St. Louis.

With the autumn comes the southward migration of ducks and geese following the traditional flyways down the rivers as they have for centuries. As if drawn by the same magnetic urge that beckons the wildfowl, the river people take their annual leave time from pushing barges to spend the short weeks of the hunting season "pushing" ducks.

They are unique characters in their own right, for the most part, rugged, jovial and fun loving. Wise in the ways of nature and the river, they are bent on enjoying life to its fullest.

On this particular day from the horizon above Nickel Swale, a lone mallard drake flies toward our blind on Big Island. Winging hard and fast, it ignores the pleading of Clyde's call and passes high above us heading for the fields west of the river.

"You'd have to make a sound like a grain of corn to get that duck's attention," he comments.

A short time later his calling ability is confirmed when three drakes and a pair of hens turn to his hailing and cup their wings to his chuckles. Three green heads end up on their backs among the decoys while the unscathed hens beat a hasty departure. Soon, three more birds are added to the bag. The brown eyed Labrador proudly retrieves them all and douses us with a healthy shake of his thick, black coat.

There follows the expected mid-morning lull between flights. Now, it's time for coffee. "Just to relieve the anticipatory quivers," as a friend once said.

Conversations in the blind run from ducks and dogs to stories of past hunts and hunters and on to the legendary women of the riverfront saloons. You get to know your hunting companions pretty well while spending a few hours in a duck blind with them.

By noon we have limited out and are back at the clubhouse pulling off our boots.

"I heard you gentlemen had a good hunt this morning." said Lewis, the club's chef, "How about a nice big hamburger and a bowl of our special chili?"

"Sounds great!"

"Thought maybe it would... Danny, three number seventeens for these here duck busters."

With pushers and cooks at gun clubs such as this, there are naturally compensation agreements and understandings of expected duties, but there is a noticeable absence of the hard-core employer/employee climate that exists at the more elegant hunting lodges. It's like comparing the atmosphere at an embassy reception with that of a local neighborhood tavern. Here the club's members, their guests, the pushers and the cooks seem to form what is more of an informal, seasonal gathering – a bonding of close-knit friends and fellow hunters.

Since bag limits were filled earlier, the afternoon is spent in the blind photographing ducks approaching, landing and taking off again. The spectacle is truly fascinating to behold.

With scenes such as this, a hunter is often faced with the questions of morals posed by those who do not hunt. Here in such tranquil moments of the quest, he may find the deep, touching moments of his relationship with the beauty and wonders of nature and of his kinship to all that is wild.

At the same time, inherited through the eons of antiquity and ancient blood lines, there exists the urge for man to prove to himself that if his life's dependency should ever be reduced to his ability to pursue and capture, he will be able to rise to the occasion and survive.

At day's end, following dinner at the Gun Club, cordials are enjoyed along with fireside tales. Soon the fresh air poisoning, contracted from hours in the duck blinds, begins to take its toll. Then, the old clubhouse is dim and quiet once more, and from out on the river the fading drone of Ted's outboard is heard as he heads for home.

* * *

THE GUN CLUB

(The preceding story first appeared in
its original form in the April/May 1988
Issue of WILDFOWL MAGAZINE. It also
won a first place award in the OUTDOOR
WRITERS OF AMERICA writing contest.)

EULOGY FOR DOUBLE L

It was the second Thursday of the month – meeting night at BJ's Rod & Gun Club. It was also half-past the libation hour when The Judge finally shuffled in and climbed aboard his permanently reserved bar stool.

"His Honor is a tad late," I noted. "Involved in anything interesting?"

"Interesting? No. Involved? Yes. For the past three weeks, I've been trying to straighten out those screwed-up cases that S.O.B. left hanging fire in my court."

The "S.O.B." referred to was a character better known as "Double L" – actually: the late L. L. Patterson, Attorney-at-Law.

There were, of course, some who had seriously mourned Double L's recent passing. But there was also a sizable number of his lesser admirers who

167

EULOGY FOR DOUBLE L

breathed a sigh of relief and allowed as to how the world had been cleansed of a curse worse than the Bubonic Plague. One of our more articulate club members went so far as to say his departure was the most rewarding event to grace mankind since the creation of the Fallopian tube.

In a way, Double L didn't really deserve such defamatory judgments. He was really a likable guy and always fun to be around, unless that is, you were the patsy for one or more of his continuous and never ending barrage of practical jokes.

It was his relentless addiction for harassing his fellow human beings that almost always caused his name to be prefaced by a variety of blasphemous adjectives. Once he found the slightest opening, he would play it to the hilt, going to extreme ends to carry out his devilish and inexhaustible torments.

"He was the most frustrating individual I've ever known," said The Judge. "At times, he would crack me up with some of his shenanigans, but then in the next instant, I'd be willing to help in causing his early demise."

There was, for example, that time when The Judge and Double L were duck hunting one afternoon. It was getting late, almost time for the expected sunset flight of mallards to arrive.

That's when Double L commenced baiting his hunting buddy with a long-

168

winded dissertation of the placement of decoys in front of their blind.

"I've been reading up on this, and it all depends on the wind direction whether the outer decoys should be hooked outward away from the main grouping or inward toward it," he lectured.

"The way I see it, with the wind coming at us like it is now, our setup is all wrong," said Double L. "I'd get out there and move a few of those 'deeks', but I've had a cramp in my leg that's givin' me fits ever since we got here."

"O.K." volunteered The Judge, "I'll do it, but you'll have to tell me how you want 'em."

Fighting his way through three feet of swamp water that rested on another foot of boot-sticking muck left The Judge gasping for breath.

"Wading through this stinking stuff is capable of leaving a man physically and mentally "non compos poopis", he choked as he picked up a couple of decoys and looked back to the blind for Double L's advice.

"Where ya want 'em?" he panted.

Double L's instructions included relocating a couple of those he had already relocated, and it left The Judge muttering comments as to what he thought Double L could do with his "hooking in and hooking out" theories.

With the water lapping near the top of his hippers, he was just before making his final placement when he heard the hushed and urgent warning from Double L.

"HEY! JUDGE... DUCKS!!! DUCKS!!! DON'T MOVE..."

In his hunched over position with arms extended and a decoy in each hand, His Honor froze as he heard the whisper of wings overhead.

The birds swung wide, but lured by Double L's soft feeding chuckle, they wheeled around for a second look. They were much lower this time, passing within a few feet of the Judge's head.

Hunkered over in this cramped and awkward position, his back was aching, but he remained as stationary as a dead stump, daring not to breathe or blink. The flight swept by him a second time but quickly banked again. Out of the corner of his eye, he watched the ducks coming in pitching from side to side with cupped wings and landing gear down.

"OH WOW!" he thought as he awaited the anticipated blasts from Double L's shotgun. "He should drop at least three of 'em!"

The wait seemed like an eternity, but all The Judge heard was the swish of wings, a muffled "quack" from a hen and the splashes of water as the whole flight settled in on the surface around him.

"What in the hell's going on?" he wondered. "Why didn't he shoot?" Within a few yards of His Honor, ducks were swimming around and babbling as they tipped up to feed the smart weed.

EULOGY FOR DOUBLE L

Ever so slowly, maybe a sixteenth of an inch at a time, His Honor rolled his eyeballs and head around just far enough to look back at the blind.

Double L was peeking out, with his impish face displaying one of his broad, chicken-eating, "How'd ya like that?", kind of grins. It was also quite obvious he was fighting back one huge eruption of laughter.

But it was when Double L read the Judge's lips slowly forming the silent words, "YOU SON-OF-A-B....", that he completely cracked-up. Loosing all control, his choking outburst caused the whole flight of ducks to jump as one bird, dousing The Judge with muddy water and almost bowling him over.

In his state of near collapse and with eyes filled with tears, Double L's three wild shots did not so much as ruffle a feather.

"I don't believe I ever felt more like shooting a man as I did that day," said The Judge finishing his tale of torment.

"Judge, you got off easy. Wait 'til I tell ya what that knuckle head did to me," volunteered "Moose" Monroe.

Eager to hear this latest indictment against Double L, the gathering at the Rod & Gun Club parted, allowing "Moose" to sidle up to the bar so he could relate the details of his misfortunes with Double L.

His story left us all talking at once. It seemed each of us had at least one or more such frustrating escapades involving Double L, and we were all trying to air the details of our own misfortunes at the same time.

Seeing that things were getting a bit out of hand, BJ immediately calmed us down. Waving his arms, he demanded silence. And, as owner of the Rod & Gun Club, he invoked his privilege to be heard.

"Now listen up, you guys," he said, when all was quiet once again. "I've been holding back on this, but I guess now is as good a time as any.

"After Double L suffered his first heart attack last year, he asked me to hold these two numbered envelopes to be opened only if and when he passed away."

The first was addressed: "To BJ And All The Gang At The Rod & Gun Club," and it contained a lengthy explanation of how the many pranks he was accused of perpetrating were all committed strictly in fun and with no malice or intention of bringing actual harm to any of his fellow hunting and fishing buddies in any way what-so-ever.

"And now," the document went on the state, "it is my final request that BJ should fill the glasses of all those present with the libations of their choice, and that said glasses shall be raised in memory of my everlasting love and friendship for each and every one of you. I'm so very honored and proud to have known you all."

With the exception of a hushed, but audible sob here and there, not a word was spoken. The Rod & Gun Club had never been so quiet as BJ complied with Double L's final wish.

At last, all was ready, and it was The Judge who first raised his glass. In quivering voice he uttered, "To Double L... May he rest in peace and his friendship be long remembered."

"To Double L," was the profound and unanimous reply.

Eventually, the conversation in the barroom slowly returned to normal but with a couple notable changes. It was all soft spoken and spaced with periods of head shaking sadness. The life of Double L was cited by many for all the good times and entertainment he had provided his fellow Rod & Gun Club members.

"You know, we're all going to miss that guy. And when you stop to think about it, things are going to be pretty damn dull around here without him," lamented Moose.

"And in his memory, I move we have an enlarged photograph of Double L framed and hung in some prominent spot here at the Rod & Gun Club.

The motion was immediately seconded by The Judge and the loud and unanimous vote approved the measure.

"Hey BJ, what was in that other envelope?" I asked, during one of the lulls.

"I don't know. It's addressed to me and it's marked, 'PERSONAL'," he answered as he opened the seal. Inside was a single sheet of paper.

With a startled look of frustration on his face, BJ handed the letter to The Judge for him to read aloud.

"Dear BJ...", it began.

"Put the drinks on my tab. I'll take care of it the next time I see you.

"Thanks...... Double L."

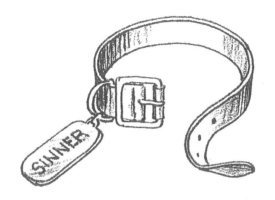

REQUIEM FOR A SINNER

First, came the stunned shock and disbelief. Then the, "Oh no!", and a throat-swelling helpless feeling. Finally there remained only the hollow epitaphs voiced by those of us who knew him.

How and why it happened was not important. The fact was, a faithful friend who had shared the pleasures, torments and triumphs of so many hunts, would be sadly missed, and future waterfowl seasons without him would never be quite the same. Now, in the hearts of his hunting companions, there would always exist a very special place reserved for him alone.

His name was "Sinner" – a black Labrador. He was still a boot-chewing pup when Art got him from the kennel, and the love affair between the two was immediate and mutual. By the time I became acquainted with him, two years later, he was a veteran retriever.

It all took place on the Illinois River near Beardstown. Art had invited us to a weekend of duck hunting at his private gun club. The Judge and I arrived in the evening just in time for libations before dinner. Art was there to greet us, and with coarse barks and a wagging tail, so was Sinner.

Returning to the hunting club each year was like a homecoming. There were the back slapping greetings from club members and the "pushers" whose friendships we had come to value highly after so many hunts together. And there was something else, too difficult to explain, but there just the same. Maybe it was the delicate whiff of burning hickory from the clubhouse fireplace. Or, perhaps it was the musty, but pleasantly clean scent emanating from the river bottom willows. But whatever it was, it welcomed us each time we came.

As always, the dinner table featured that "below the salt" kind of atmosphere with the bantering and laughter of real down-to-earth people setting the scene. Then, following our meal, it was cordials, soft music and easy chairs in the hypnotic glow of dying embers as treasured memories of past hunts and hunters were recalled.

This part of the evening was short lived however, for the "fresh air poisoning" from the long day's hunt and the promise of an early morning wake-up soon lured nodding heads and weary bodies to warm blankets and comfortable beds.

All too soon, the roaring voice of the club manager, Ted Jamison, was reminding us, "There's no way you're going to shoot at any ducks if you're going to sleep all day."

The grumbling complaints and threats of Ted's early demise eventually gave way to the continuation of the hilarities of the previous evening.

When we stepped from the clubhouse to taste the crisp November morning, a pale moon and a few die hard stars were just beginning to fade. Sinner was waiting with excited barks and a happy tail as he bounded back and forth between us and the boat dock. Soon his thick, black coat was rippling in the wind as he stood in the bow of our speeding johnboat.

Once the craft's flat bottom grounded out on a shallow water covered island of brush and smart weed, our hunting day began in earnest. It was all stumble and cussing as we waded the last hundred yards through a foot of blue mud, ten inches of water and a half inch of breaking ice. By the time we reached the far side overlooking the wide expanse of Swango's Swale, our shins were bruised and we were gulping heavily.

Before we could recoup, our torture was renewed in front of the duck blind as we broke out the decoys from the frozen surface. With that cotton-spitting task completed we crawled into our camouflaged hide gasping for breath, and beneath our heavy clothes, our perspiring bodies began to shake as the cold found its way through layers of insulation. To help warm us both, Sinner pressed close against my left hip boot.

"This is what makes duck huntin' so damned much fun... I guess," panted Art, as he pushed shells in the magazine of his twelve gauge automatic. "The way everything is iced over this morning, we'll be lucky if we even see a duck."

He was wrong. Before his last shell clicked into place, there was a sudden swishing of wings overhead as five mallards surprised us from behind the blind. They climbed out fast and high, swinging wide over the back waters.

Ted gave them a comeback call and they turned, but they were still too high on their second pass. Then his soft feeding chuckle banked them into the wind and they locked their wings.

Two shots sounded as one followed by a third. A pair of green-heads crashed into the broken ice among the decoys, while the others quickly departed for safer and quieter climes. Before that third shot sounded, Sinner was out of the blind, and he brought both birds back on the same trip.

"Way to go, Sinner!" complimented Art, patting the dog's head. The gesture was acknowledged by a vigorous shake that caught us all in a spray of muddy water.

"It's amazing how a flight of ducks can warm things up," said Ted. "Anyone for coffee?"

He was pouring the steaming brew into the lid of a thermos when, mysteriously, out of nowhere, a flight of mallards was hanging above the decoys right in front of us. There was a furious scramble in the blind with everything going wrong.

The coffee was spilled. The barrel of one shotgun became entangled in the blind's chicken wire and smart weed camouflage. Another was touched off before it was solidly shouldered and cheeked, and its shot string went wide of its mark. The third gun swung in a perfect lead on a passing drake, but the safety was still locked in the "on" position.

The entire flight of at least a dozen birds escaped without so much as a ruffled feather. In the blind everyone was yakking at the same time.

With the report of that single shot, Sinner was into the icy water and muck again. This time, there was nothing for him to retrieve, and he returned with his head and tail down.

Climbing back up in the blind, he drenched us with another shake, and the look he gave us demanded our apology.

"Sorry about that, Ol' Buddy," I sighed, rubbing his ears.

Following that last fiasco, activity slowed considerably. A warming sun brought an end to the thin ice, and a gentle breeze rocked life into the decoys. Conditions in the blind were much improved, and Sinner leaned against my leg with his head down and his eyes half closed.

Silence usually dominates such periods, with each hunter deeply entranced in his own private thoughts as he scans the horizons for the unpredictable flights. What little conversation there is comes in the form of reminiscing. Good-time stories of past hunts and hunters and dogs are recalled only to be followed once again by more profound and quiet thoughts.

I was in the middle of my third round of "she loves me, she loves me not", as I plucked leaves from the blind's smart weed cover, when Ted's duck call drew our attention to a squadron of mallards winging high over the far side of open water. They turned toward our set of blocks and he enticed them closer with a muffled chuckle.

The shots that followed dumped two drakes in the decoys and a third farther out. The far duck had a broken wing and was thrashing about on the surface.

Sinner passed up the two dead birds and bounded after the cripple. As he approached it, the duck dived out of sight. Sinner stopped, looking around, trying to spot his quarry. From our higher position the blind, we saw the duck come up several yards away.

REQUIEM FOR A SINNER

"Hey, Sinner!" yelled Art, waving his arm. "Back, Sinner, Back!"

The lab looked in the direction of Art's hand signal and was after the drake in an instant. Another dive by the duck, another signal from Art and Sinner had his crippled duck.

On the way back to the blind he picked up the second mallard. Then, with his mouth filled, he nosed the third ahead as he waded in. Beautiful! A triple retrieve!

Later, while Ted and Sinner were out looking for a hard-hit bird that had glided into the far woods, Art, The Judge, and I were caught off guard by a pair of green-heads. They slipped in on us fast, making a quick turn with their necks down as they gave our decoys the once over.

Two shotguns and a camera came up, and two quick shots splashed the drakes in the water at the outer edge of our blocks.

"Well, which one of us is going to make like a retriever and go pick 'em up?" asked Art.

"Since our photographer friend wants to record this for the archives, I guess it's up to you or me," said The Judge. "Pick a number - one, two or three."

"Two," returned Art.

"Take your shotgun along so you'll look more like a hunter than a dog," said The Judge without revealing his number.

REQUIEM FOR A SINNER

Muttering something about voting for a different judge come next election, Art waded out through the shallow water and calf deep muck.

From the blind, I zoomed in to catch his hammed-up smile as he posed holding up the ducks in one hand and his shotgun in the other. But, when he took his first step toward the blind, his left foot stuck hopelessly in the mud, and his forward momentum carried him right out of his boot.

Art, his smile, the ducks and his shotgun all ended up flat in a splash of water, muck and smart weed. I caught the whole mess in a series of photos.

Ted and Sinner had returned with the lost duck just in time to witness it all. And, as Art sat in the blind ringing out his socks, Sinner watched with a cocked head and raised ears. The Judge and I will both swear to this day that dog was actually smiling.

In the boat on the way back to the clubhouse that evening, Sinner sat resting his head on Art's knee.

"Hello, Ol' Brown Eyes," crooned Art, rubbing the dog's neck. "You did real great today, Sinner. I'm real proud of you."

The oral conversation may have been one-sided, but words were unnecessary. A dog's eyes have a way of expressing his thoughts, and it was quite obvious from the looks the two exchanged, they knew exactly what the other was thinking.

REQUIEM FOR A SINNER

There is a bond between hunters and their dogs that is very special. While a household pet may be lovable and often thought of as a family member, a gunning dog, like Sinner, is more than just that.

He is a true companion joining actively in the excitements, the hardships and the satisfactions of the hunt. But, there is more – much more. A personal closeness exists between the two, an understanding and feeling for the same sense of values along with the cares, the joys and moods one shares with the other.

Such dogs can make lasting impressions on a person's life. Sinner was certainly one that did. Over the years there have been other such dogs – Chester, Sam, Bullet, Phydeaux. Each, in his own way became, and will remain, a part of us.

With Sinner sitting beside him that evening, as our boat moved into the sunset, I was sure Art had already reserved a special corner in his heart for this very special friend.

Somehow, I believe Sinner knew that, too.

* * *

This story first appeared in "HUNT FOREVER" magazine, a publication of SAFARI CLUB INTERNATIONAL.

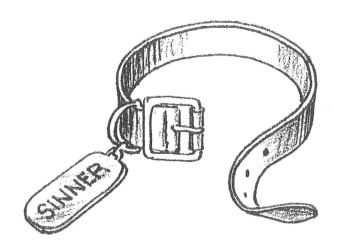

PART III

OF PONDERING AND PORTAGING

"What a man finally becomes, how he adjusts to his world, is a composite of all the horizons he has experienced."

Sigurd F. Olson

THE COURTIN' BRIDGE

Little had changed since the old man's last visit, and that was as it should be, for there must always be places such as this. Quiet, unhurried places, where time slumbers while waiting for the past to catch up and where history and memories stroll hand in hand through a picturesque countryside.

All but forgotten in today's world where lives are cluttered with busy schedules and regulated by computers, Parke County, Indiana abounds in scenic beauty. It is a land of rolling hills, rocky ravines and miles of meandering streams, and is best known for its covered bridges – more than thirty of them – the largest concentration to be found anywhere in the world. Some were built more than a century ago.

THE COURTIN' BRIDGE

Rooted here were memories of his youth – precious memories of barefoot summers and cool, refreshing swims in Raccoon Creek near the Jackson Bridge, and of boyhood dreams rising in the smoke of a driftwood campfire on a sand bar in Sugar Creek near the Turkey Run Narrows Bridge. More than seventy years had passed since that boy of twelve carved his initials in the Burr arch of the Roseville Bridge spanning Big Raccoon Creek, and the old man found them again today.

His visit took him to the Thorpe Ford Bridge built in 1912 by J.A. Britton. As he stood beneath its portal, a quiver of depression and loneliness swept over him, and a tear rolled down his furrowed cheek. For him, this place held the most cherished memories of all. On a day, long years ago, a kiss was shared by a young couple as they carried their school books through its shaded tunnel. He had married that girl, and for them, this would forever be their very own courtin' bridge.

Farther on, he finds the charred timbers of the once beautiful, "Big Red". The bridge, near Rosedale, was in daily use for 96 years before its 248 foot span was destroyed by a gang of vandals. The requiem for its loss is shared by many.

Thomas Edison was putting the finishing touches on his first light bulb when J.J. Daniels of Rockville began construction of this nostalgic old bridge, and it came to be known affectionately, as, "Big Red". For the old man's friend, Max Lee and his family, its burning was a tragic loss, much like the passing of a long loved friend and valued neighbor.

"We often hunted quail near that bridge," the old man remembered. "And, one day, we found a small stand of "bluestem" nearby. It is the only remaining remnants of the tall grasses dating back to the days of the buffalo."

Now, the prairie bluestem, the buffalo, the Big Red Bridge, Max Lee, and... yes, even that girl he had married were all gone. He sighed, choking back a cry and sadly shaking his head as he slowly walked away.

The cornerstone at the south abutment of the Jackson Bridge reminded him that it was erected in 1861, the year Abe Lincoln became President and the Civil War began. The bridge is still in use today.

His wanderings now took him to the 317 foot, double span, West Union Bridge crossing Sugar Creek. It, too, was built by J.J. Daniels in 1876, about the same time the Souix were closing in on George Custer's 7th Cavalry at the Little Big Horn.

"It's a wonder any of these old crossings are still here today," the old man muttered. "What a marvelous feat of engineering it took for them to last this long."

THE COURTIN' BRIDGE

The historic old structures were designed to withstand the elements. They were roofed with cedar shingles to protect the wooden flooring and support timbers from the weather. They were built rugged enough to survive wind, hail and flood. But, a galloping horse could set up vibrations that would often weaken the joints and trusses.

This is why the portals leading into the old spans still bear the warning for riders and drivers of wagons and buggies to, "CROSS THIS BRIDGE AT A WALK". With the coming of the automobile, "SOUND HORN" signs were added; warning oncoming traffic someone was already passing through its dark tunnel.

A visit to covered bridge country is a return to rural life as it once was. The back roads lead past log cabins, split rail fences, working grist mills and old country stores. It is like stumbling back into an age found only in faded paintings and fireside legends. Here calendars seem to have been laid aside, for seasons are far more important than months, and lives are seldom dominated by dates and deadlines.

SPRING... arrives with the green-up and the time for planning and planting. Streams, flowing beneath the old covered bridges, will be running full with the run-off of winter's melt and early season rains. Throughout the hills, redbuds and dogwoods will be blending their pinks and whites with the budding greenery of the hardwoods.

Along creek banks, a warming sun graces the faces of tiny dog-tooth violets, spring beauties and Dutchman's breeches. Mysteriously, overnight, yellow morels come to play their games of hide-n-seek among the leaves of May-apples. All is new and young, and the freshness is filled with the sound of birdsong.

SUMMER... the streams are clear and the hours belonged to a small boy with a willow pole, a kite string line and a corncob bloat as he fishes from the bank of the old pond.

A variety of small sunfish made up his catch, for tackle-breaking bass are not often found in these waters. And maybe that, too, is in keeping with such a storybook setting as this. Who cares how many you catch or how large they are when it's the experience one remembers?

AUTUMN... the time of harvesting both crops and color. A spectacular beauty blankets the hills and woodlands, igniting them in blazing hues of crimson, gold and copper. Their glories could challenge the painter's palette and dumb the tongues of poets. As if it were answering a call to vespers, the long walks of evening are companioned with quiet and sacred questions of, "How?" and "Why?" and with the insignificance of your being.

THE COURTIN' BRIDGE

Pioneer activities come to life once more as friends and visitors relive the age of quilting bees, rail-splitting and corn-husking. And with hopes of winning turkeys, hams and sides of bacon, the sharp cracks of muzzle loading rifles send round lead balls to an X carved cedar shake.

White clouds of smoke rising from burning hickory beneath copper kettles, bring the promise of apple butter, and from the wood-burning stoves of country kitchens come the mouth-watering aromas of baking corn bread and pumpkin pies.

WINTER... snows clothe the hills and valleys in a white mantle of silence and the old covered bridges are bathed in the soft glow of moonlight. The merry jingle of sleigh bells are heard and the voices of skaters rise in harmony, as the gather around warming fires on the banks of frozen mill ponds.

If the etchings of Currier and Ives could ever come to life, it would surely take place here and now.

In late winter, when the sap begins to flow, tap pails will be seen on the sides of maple trees. And, from the sugar camps where syrup is born, there will come that wonderful flavor to compliment a breakfast of flapjacks and country sausage.

Yes, seasons come and go in this land of covered bridges just as they do everywhere else, but here, life today is much as it was yesterday, and somehow you know tomorrow is not going to change that. For here, where time itself seems timeless, the past has collided with the present and come out the winner.

And, through it all, for the old man, there will always be that most wonderful memory of all – that long ago kiss in the tunnel of their courtin' bridge.

EVEN GEORGE DID IT

Long rays of early morning sunlight
filter through the mist hovering over a
river in the Ontario bush country.
Only the distant lamenting of a loon
and the soft lap of water against the
bow intrudes upon the perfect
stillness. Ahead, on a shoreline
point, a doe and fawn pose like statues
as my canoe glides quietly toward them.
The vista creates a mood of complete
tranquility and should be recorded.

I rest my paddle across the gunwales
and pick up my camera. But as I focus
on the scene, I hear my voice utter an
involuntary, **"DAMN!"**

Beyond and above the deer, the rock
bluff background spoils the picture.
There, on its granite wall, in three
foot white spray-painted letters is,
"TROOP 29".

195

EVEN GEORGE DID IT

This little drama took place several years ago, but it is as disturbing today as it was then. For it is far from being uncommon and certainly not anything new. From the age when he made a cave his home, man has been driven by some unexplainable urge to paint, scratch, carve and gouge his mark on some kind of surface to let those who were to come later know that he had been there before them.

At Natural Bridge in Virginia, when he was a young surveyor, the father of our country saw fit to carve his "G.W." on its stone abutment. For someone who had reportedly tested his hatchet on a perfectly good cherry tree, maybe this was to be expected. Those initials, however, have become a shrine and are now as much a part of the tourist attraction as the work of nature itself.

The same was said to have taken place a few years later in Kentucky, when a well know frontiersman described one of his hair-raising adventures when he carved: "D. BOONE KILT A BAR ON THIS TREE".

At El Moro, in New Mexico, Spanish conquistadors and later, the pioneers of passing wagon trains left their names all over the sides of a whole mountain. It is now a National Monument.

The timbers of hundred year old covered bridges in Parke County, Indiana have recorded a myriad of past events, such as: "JOHN LOVES MARY",

EVEN GEORGE DID IT

"CLYDE x TOOTSIE", all the characters in the Greek alphabet and the dates of every high school graduating class from 1900 through the turn of this century and beyond.

During World War II, there were but few places on the face of the globe where Kilroy was not.

All of this may lead a person to wonder what our astronauts left on the moon besides their footprints and a pile of discarded junk from their space vehicle.

Recently, when I was fly-fishing the upper reaches of the Magalloway River in northwestern Maine, and some 14 miles from the nearest logging road, my backcast somehow became attracted to a tree limb. Mumbling a radically different version of the Rosary, I reeled up my slack line as I waded for shore. When I was freeing my Coachman from the offending branch, I happened to glance down at the granite slab beneath my feet.

There, permanently embedded in the great stone, was a bronze tablet inscribed:

"This Marks The Area Where

PRESIDENT DWIGHT D. EISENHOWER

Fished in June, 1955

* * *

EVEN GEORGE DID IT

Erected by the Maine Federation of

Republican Women, 1970"

I had come to the Magalloway to "get away from it all", but somehow my fantasy of escaping from people, pollution and politicians, to fish in an unspoiled wilderness, was abruptly shattered.

Add to all of this the graffiti found on the walls of johns, phone booths, bus stations or whatever, and one may begin to speculate that such a thing as a clean, unmarked surface of any kind may soon be making the endangered list.

From mountain peaks to barrow pits, from back-alley fences to capitol domes, all around the world, in every language and script, in primitive petroglyphs and in artistic masterpieces, man has seen fit to make his presence known. Human made structures and nature's own have felt the blades and tasted the dyes used by these recording historians.

What is it that moves people to perform such deeds?

Surely the psych boys have their theories, of what worth they may be. Regardless of their explanation, the clutter is a tasteless and distracting mess wherever it appears. But, when it disfigures some object of our natural environment, the cut is more unkind than that of Brutus. What is even less understandable is the fact that we not only seem to condone such acts but apparently go to the extreme of promoting and glamorizing them.

Statues of our historical heroes in parks or on village squares and courthouse lawns, are fitting tributes to both the individuals and to the talents of the sculptor. But, wounding the natural beauty and grandeur of a mountain, as was done at Rushmore, is going just a tad too far.

Not to be outdone by the "damn Yankees", the South committed their own sins at Stone Mountain, Georgia, where they have displayed the images of the great Confederate leaders.

Even now, so that our Native American brothers will receive equal acclaim, Chief Crazy Horse AND his noble steed are being chiseled in relief on the side of yet another mountain in South Dakota. It is said the work of the artist will become immortal. The beauty of the mountain in its natural state, unfortunately will not.

All of this must someday, somehow, come to a screeching halt. We are getting more and more heroes and fewer unblemished mountains.

It is entirely possible that what little our expanding progress may leave undefiled and in its natural state, future populations, with their chisels, jack hammers and blasting caps will not long overlook.

Today, the question, "How much wilderness is enough?", is often posed by those who seek to exploit the planet Earth of its resources for profit and personal gain.

The answer to this question is obvious.

Our wilderness and our natural wonders go hand in hand. And, when such splendors move us to ponder our own insignificance and the very state of our being, then there can be no question as to how much is enough. For what better legacy could we pass on to future generations than such a precious and priceless heritage as this?

* * *

This story first appeared in its original form in the Summer 1986 issue of OUTDOOR AMERICA, the magazine of the IZAAK WALTON LEAGUE OF AMERICA.

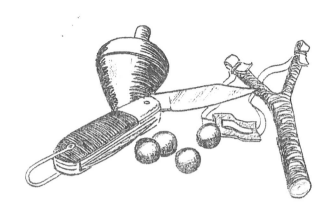

ONCE THERE WAS A BOY

*"A boy's will is the winds will,
And the thoughts of youth are
long, long thoughts."*

from "My Lost Youth" by
Henry Wadsworth Longfellow

It was summer, the best time of all to be a young boy free of long dreary months of being imprisoned behind a school desk. Pint-sized, towheaded, with a cowlick and a few scattered freckles, he was a barefoot adventure in bib overalls looking for a place to happen. And, here at Grandma Jenuine's farm, was where he would most likely find it.

All those boring lessons and dull textbooks were behind him now — at least for a while. So too, were those raps across his knuckles when Ol' Miss

201

ONCE THERE WAS A BOY

Reinhardt's hickory pointer returned his wandering mind to the classroom and away from the daydreams he found in the view from the schoolhouse window.

But, all of that was yesterday. Today, at Grandma's farm, the world belonged to him. His activities followed his whims of the moment and his pace rivaled that of the turtle. Plans were never made; they just somehow evolved, and if he ran out of time doing whatever, well... there was always tomorrow.

Here, he was in a different kind of school – one he dearly loved. Its roof was the open sky, and its walls the surrounding hills and woodlands. Nature was his teacher, and all of its mysteries were the studies he loved most.

When his "How's" and "Why's" demanded explanations to a myriad of important questions, he always turned to Uncle Ed, who, he knew for sure, was the smartest man in the whole world.

On a sunny morning, with an old Prince Albert tobacco can of red worms tucked in the bib pocket of his overalls, he was off to catch "Ol' Bucket-mouth". That's what Uncle Ed called the legendary, line-breakin' monster of a bass everyone knew dwelled in the depths of the old mill pond.

The dusty lane led him to where giant oaks and hickories surrounded the water's edge. With the butt of his willow pole jammed in the mud and his worm baited line in the water, he lolled in the shade, belly down, resting on his elbows with his palms cupping his cheeks. As he watched his corncob float drifting lazily on the surface, his dreams carried him far away to some wherever land.

More often than not, his day's experience would far outweigh his catch. But there were a few occasions when his eyes danced with excitement as he proudly returned to Grandma's kitchen with a dripping mess of nice bluegills strung on a willow branch.

On many a clear evening, he would lie on his back in the sweet smelling clover as he counted stars overhead. They seemed so close he could almost hear them twinkling, and he made his secret wishes upon those rare ones that shot across the sky.

At other times, he would climb among the branches of that old elm tree and listen to the voices of the night. He came to recognize the cricket, the locust and the katydid, and with practice, he learned to imitate the calls of the hootie-owl and the whippoorwill.

Then there were those afternoons, following a cool dip in the "crick". He would lie on the sandbar under the old covered bridge, and his dreams meandered with the music of the rippling water. Sometimes, he used his old Barlow knife to carve his initials on a small stick and drop it on the riffles. It would drift away, spinning a few turns on an eddy before disappearing around a bend, and it always left him wondering to what strange and enchanting land it would be carried and how someday, maybe he would even go there.

On other days, he whistled with the meadow larks as he wandered across the meadow back of the farm. Although he had learned to expect it, his heart invariably skipped a beat when that same covey of quail flushed from under his feet near the place where the pasture joined the woods.

He was never without his hickory slingshot protruding from the hip pocket of his overalls. It offered him a comforting feeling of assurance and security. After all, who knew what dangers he may encounter while exploring the shadows of the hardwood forest?

His youthful imagination conjured up visions of everything from black bears to bobcats. Or perhaps, he would even meet the spirits of the Indians who once roamed these parts.

And, why not? Had he not recently found a small, flint arrowhead beside the brook, and had not Uncle Ed told him the late evening fog, hovering above the lowlands was really smoke from their campfires?

Deep in the woods was a sinkhole and the entrance to a limestone cavern. Uncle Ed warned him he must never go inside because he could get lost in there and never be found. He also said, Jesse James and his outlaw band was said to have buried gold somewhere in the cave's dark passages, and supposedly, it was still there, guarded by the ghosts of those old train robbers.

The boy knew for sure this was a fact, too, 'cause once he had pussy-footed up to the cave's sinister opening and called Jesse's name, and he heard their haunting voices from the darkness far inside, repeating it over and over.

One day, Uncle Ed took him to a high bluff overlooking the broad river valley.

"Down there," he pointed, "is where the old buffalo trace crossed the Wabash River. Back in those days, there were thousands of those big, shaggy critters around here. Now, they're all gone like so many other things."

Near where they stood on the bluff, they found the old cornerstones that once supported the log cabin belonging to the boy's great grandfather.

"What a view! The old man could not have picked a better place to build his home," praised Uncle Ed. "Over the years, there were twenty-one kids raised in that cabin.

"Your mother grew up here, and she told me when she was a little girl, she used to sit on a log and hold a brass mold while her Pa filled it with molten lead to make bullets for his muzzle-loading rifle.

ONCE THERE WAS A BOY

"He must have brought a passel of vittles to the table when he hunted with that ol' smoke-pole."

The very next day, when the two walked to the woods together, Uncle Ed was carrying something long and heavy rolled up in a blanket. It was the very same cap and ball rifle he had spoken of the day before.

The boy watched with mounting excitement as Uncle Ed poured a measure of black powder in the muzzle. Then he wrapped a greased patch around a lead ball and tamped it down the barrel with the hickory ramrod.

"You're next in the family to own this," he said, "so I reckon it's high time you learned how to shoot it." He rested the rifle across a log and spread the blanket on the ground for the boy to lie on.

Then, Uncle Ed helped him to shoulder and cheek the tiger-striped, maple stock and sight down the long barrel at a cedar shingle he had placed against the high creek bank about fifty yards away. When he was told to slowly squeeze the trigger, there was a loud roar and a cloud of white smoke that scared the boy more than he ever remembered being before.

This long, hunk of metal and wood he was holding had suddenly come to life in a way the boy could have never believed possible. The experience was, without a doubt, the greatest thrill of his young life, and he was even more elated when he saw the black hole in that cedar shake.

Even though his cheek was red and he was rubbing his shoulder, his dancing eyes and broad smile told Uncle Ed how much this truly meant to him. Now he was being treated like a man, but a small part of him would always be that boy.

* * *

Many years later, a tear was glistening in the eyes of an old man, as he sat resting on the stump of the old elm tree he remembered so well. He felt so very tired and so very much alone, and he sadly shook his head.

The deserted and weather-beaten old farmhouse in front of him was almost hidden among the tall weeds and brambles. Its front door sagged on one hinge, and most of the windows were broken out.

"It was all so long ago," he muttered to himself. "Grandma, Uncle Ed, the farm, they are all gone now. Old Hank Longfellow had it figured right. Now, only the memories are left."

207

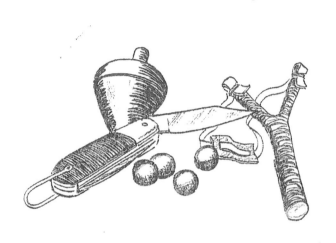

FLYING LOW AND SLOW

Once upon a television station, I co-hosted a weekly, half-hour outdoor program together with one of my fishing buddies, J. "Catfish" Ennis. It was back in the days when TV was still in its infancy – the dark ages – you might say. You know, all black and white presentations and live on camera. We did, however, eventually graduate to color and taped programming.

Actually, ours was one of the very first televised outdoor shows in the whole country, and it continued for 21 years before we became old, ugly and stupid all at the same time and decided to quit while we were ahead.

Looking back on it all, we did have some exciting times doing it and came away with enough memories to fill a lifetime.

FLYING LOW AND SLOW

Producing films and gathering story material for our "TV SPROTSMAN'S SHOW" not only took us to many of the prime fishing and hunting areas in the United States but also to the steaming jungles of Central America, the rivers and lakes of the Canadian bush country, and even to the vast expanses beyond the tree line, in the Arctic.

Together, we shared countless pleasures and adventures with few disagreements. Well... come to think about it, there was one little ol' thing that occasionally gouged me like a loose fishhook in the hip pocket of a pair of tight jeans.

Each time we climbed into a floatplane flying to some remote fishing area, Catfish always insisted on riding in the copilot's seat. He constantly reminded me that his wartime flying experience was far more thorough than mine. After all, I was only a foxhole Marine in the Pacific while he, on the other hand, had been a barber at an Air Force base in Iceland.

"I can help navigate, and in case something should go wrong, I'll be there to assist," was his argument.

Bowing to this professionalism, and in the interest of flying safety, I always ended up in the rear baggage compartment of the plane, with an assortment of fishing and camp gear, as I tried to fit my carcass, comfortably, on top of an outboard motor's gas tank with its interesting metal carrying handle and fuel line cleats.

FLYING LOW AND SLOW

From time to time, Catfish would look back, feeding me bits of information of the progress of our flight. On the many trips we made together, his voice shouting above the noise of the engine, took on a ring of authority and calm reassurance.

Even his, "Don't worry, I think we can make it," had a comforting ring to it, even though I had not the foggiest idea what I was supposed to be worried about.

Once in a while, on rare and flattering occasions, my personal advice was sought in making decisions relating to our flight. Like that time, for instance, when we were ready to take off in a Cessna floatplane. With its engine idling, the plane was rocking in the chop of a shallow bay of a remote lake in the northern Ontario bush country.

"The pilot wants to know if there are any rocks or submerged logs up ahead," my fearless copilot yelled over his shoulder.

"None that I know of..." I answered from my perch on top of the gas can. But, the rest of my sentence: "I've never been on this lake before", was lost in the roar and rattle as the plane shot down the bay at full throttle.

Just before we ran out of lake, the Cessna finally lifted clear of the water, and the left float clipped a couple of twigs from the top branch of a tall spruce on the shoreline. Ennis

211

looked back, giving me the old, "index finger-to-thumb", OK sign that I had done good.

Most of the time, however, it was his experienced opinion that carried the weight. Once, in the Northwest Territories, we were preparing to fly from the fishing lodge to a river outpost up near the Arctic coast. When we walked down to the dock, we found our sad-faced pilot leaning against an equally sad looking single engine Norseman. Both pilot and plane appeared to have seen better years long before Ben Franklin began flying kites. We counted the empty holes in the scavenged instrument panel. Only the oil pressure gauge and a stuck compass remained.

"Hum! Looks like a punch-board with only two chances left," Ennis appraised, "but I think it'll get us there and back."

The flight to the outpost camp was uneventful, although once we were airborne and on course, "Ol' Sleepy" turned things over to his copilot and appeared to take a nap. Meanwhile, a rather pale and wide-eyed Catfish Jack white-knuckled the steering gear in a panic frozen grip. Thankfully, "Sleepy" took over the controls again in time to find our destination through the scattered patches of fog hanging over the water.

It was what happened on the return trip the next day that caused our drowsy pilot to raise his ears and eyebrows like a tired coon hound.

It all came about as we were shuddering and shaking our way up river as we picked up speed for our take-off. A sudden mushroom of black smoke, followed by a couple of flames licking out from under the cowl, prompted "Ol' Sleepy" to bring everything to a sputtering stop.

"Hummm!" he mused.

Kneeling on the pontoons, Ennis and I canoe paddled the Norseman over to the river bank. An inspection revealed a blackened hole burnt through the rusty manifold exhaust under the cowl.

That was when "Sleepy" displayed his hidden talents as a resourceful bush pilot. Repairs were made utilizing an empty tomato can retrieved from the dump back of the outpost tent. This was split down the side and padded with a piece of asbestos, pilfered from around the smoke stack that kept the tent from catching fire. It was all held in place, around the blown out pipe, with a couple of twisted coat hangers, also found at the outpost tent.

Later, when we arrived at the dock back at the lodge, we checked the repair job again. The blistered tomato can was just before burning through.

"Amazing!" I exclaimed.

"Worked, didn't it?" mumbled "Sleepy" as he shuffled up to the lodge for a cup of coffee.

FLYING LOW AND SLOW

Experiences such as this left me with mixed emotions as to how much of a help Catfish would be, "in case something went wrong".

However, since the whole fiasco resulted with nothing more than a near coronary on my part, I was destined to keep my keester on the gas can in the rear of the plane.

However, there was one other occasion, when my confidence in my copilot's expertise as a navigator and tour guide was once again tarnished just a tad.

This time it was on a trip up to a tree like lake near the Arctic Circle with friends Pete and Fred, a couple of other idiots from our home town who decided to go along with us.

We arrived by jet at a small mining settlement in northern Manitoba. It was sort of a transportation hub, and evidently the jumping-off place to destinations farther north.

The little terminal building was jammed with people. Miners, Indians, Eskimos, prospectors, trappers and fishermen were arriving and departing or just hanging around watching those who were. Utter confusion dominated the scene. The contents in a tub of night crawlers at a live bait shop would have been better organized.

"Where do we go to get our floatplane?" I wondered aloud, as we stood there with our pile of duffel bags and rod cases.

FLYING LOW AND SLOW

"I'll check it out," said Catfish, shouldering his way over to a desk where a girl was searching a typewriter for the right key to peck.

"I beg your pardon, Miss," he said. "We have just arrived, and we are supposed to fly out to a fishing camp up on Grayling Lake. Can you tell us where we..."

"Just pile your gear on that cart over there," she interrupted. "As soon as they finish fueling your plane, you can go out and load up. There's your pilot," she gestured to a bearded young man watching the fueling operation from a window overlooking the runway. The plane being readied was a big De Havilland Otter equipped with huge, low-pressure tires.

As we introduced ourselves to the pilot, I asked, "Aren't we supposed to fly up to Grayling Lake in a floatplane?"

"How many are in your party?" asked the pilot, ignoring my query.

"Four," replied Catfish.

"Hummm! That will make eleven of us all together, counting the others going up on the same flight, but I guess we can make it. The strip up there is a little soft and kind of short, but I've been in there with some lumber a couple of times, so I think we'll be OK."

"We'll be OK," Catfish repeated to us in his reassuring voice.

"But, where's the floatplane?" I pressed. Once again I was ignored.

FLYING LOW AND SLOW

About an hour later, the Otter broke through a scud of low rain clouds, and there, right on target, was the island. From the edge of the shoreline, and running inland to the edge of a huge quagmire, was the shortest landing strip we had ever seen. With full flaps down and the stall warning buzzer screaming, our plane made its approach just above the water.

"It may be a little rough, so hang on," yelled Ennis from his copilot's seat.

We touched down, bounced, and touched again. The plane shot up over a hump and nosed down on the other side before dropping to a jolting halt at the very edge of the swamp. Pete crossed himself. Fred sat there with both eyes tightly closed and a firm grip on the seat. The other passengers were bug-eyed and gasping for breath, except for one who was boozed up and oblivious to it all. He applauded, and that's when our fearless copilot rose from his seat and took a bow.

As I stood watching our fishing tackle and duffle bags being unloaded, the fishermen who had just completed their week's stay at the camp were gathered nearby waiting to fly out for home.

"How's the fishin'?!" I asked one of them.

"It's really pretty good," he answered. "But that camp is something else. The food's lousy, the cabins and

216

boats all leak like the inside of a minnow bucket, and the guides are drunk most of the time. I wouldn't recommend this place to anyone."

"That's strange," I said. "I've always heard that Jim Auston ran a pretty good camp."

"Oh! You're talking about Nakomic Lodge. It's up at the other end of the lake, about 20 miles from here. It's a real nice place. I wish that's where we would have gone instead of making reservations at this dump. You have to fly to Auston's in a floatplane."

"Guess what!" I said to Ennis when he walked up.

Thinking back, on all of my years of flying low and slow in the bush planes, if I had it to do over again, I believe I'd do things a little differently. Like purchasing lifetime subscriptions to a couple of good aviation magazines, and perhaps making a donation or two to some bush pilot's retirement home.

Maybe, just maybe, that would have qualified me to challenge Catfish for the right to that copilot's seat. At least once in a while.

MS. DIAMONDS AND THE OUTDOOR WRITER

*"I have no doubt the devil grins
as seas of ink I splatter.
May God forgive my literary sins.
The other kind don't matter."*

– Robert Service

EAT... SLEEP... and SEX: The three basic functions of man. Any additional functions create specialization.

For example: Add <u>FISHING and HUNTING</u>, and your man suddenly becomes an "outdoorsman".

Now, let's take it one step farther: add <u>WRITING</u>. Now your entity has a new title: A critter known as an outdoor writer.

About now, someone is sure to scream, "HOW DID OUR WORLD GO SO WRONG?"

More often than not, the "screamer" will be someone you meet at times and places least expected. Usually, it's someone who is an expert at screaming, not much for doing, but at the same time, unshakably set in their argumentative ways. Before you realize it, you will be defending yourself and your personal interests against hopeless odds.

It's kinda like getting into a urinating contest with a skunk. There's no way you can win.

So much for a lesson in social science!

* * *

Pet and I met Bill and Penny last spring at a Ducks Unlimited Sponsor Banquet, and we hit it off from the very start. Pet and Penny find they belong to the same national sorority (albeit different universities).

As it happens, Bill and I also have a couple of things in common (also with a touch of an albeit). He likes to fish and hunt. So do I. He likes beer and Scotch. So do I. He's a millionaire... That's where our similarities end.

Anyway, it came as quite a surprise a few weeks later, when we received an invitation from our new friends to a dinner party they were hosting at their country club. Pet was all excited. She loves formal dinner parties.

I hate them. Usually, among other things, the only people we'll know are the host and hostess who have invited us.

Penny greets us when we arrive and immediately leads Pet away and introduces her to a group of her lady friends. Left alone, I look around for Bill but fail to spot him. In fact, all of the male guests seem to be gathered in their own little cliques, and they are complete strangers to me.

However, a friendly bartender makes me feel at home by plying his trade. So, with drink in hand, I leisurely stroll to the hors d'oeuvre table. Being of the chip and dip class, I am amazed at such a spread of elegance.

Beside a beautiful, ice sculpture centerpiece is a large silver tray heaped with cocktail shrimp. In fact, the table is loaded with a whole passel of enticing morsels, the names and origins of which I hadn't the foggiest. But, not being in the adventurous mood at the moment, I opt for the shrimp.

As I am helping myself to a second go at them, I become aware of someone beside me also picking at some of the assorted goodies. She is blonde, frizzy-haired, fiftyish and humming to herself while daintily holding her wine glass by the stem with three overly jeweled fingers extended to the side.

MS. DIAMONDS AND THE OUTDOOR WRITER

I suddenly remembered a long departed fishing buddy and how he would more than likely have sized her up: "All tits and diamonds and as phony as a virgin in a brothel."

"Nice party," I say, not wishing to ignore her completely.

"Simply lAHvely," she croons. "William and Penelope always host the most gAHgeous affairs."

I introduce myself, and she turns. Over the top of her gem crested half-glasses, she studies me through her thickly mascaraed lashes.

"Ooh, yes! I am told you are one of THOSE," she cringes in a revolting tone.

"Which one of THOSE?" I question with raised eye brows.

"They say you hunt and fish and even go so far as to glamorize such atrocities in your written works. It is completely beyond my comprehension how you can possibly have the intestinal fortitude to actually murder those poor fish and AHnimals.

"Neither do I understand why anyone of sound mind would lower themselves to read about such dreadful habits."

"Some like diamonds – some like trout streams," I countered with a shrug.

Ignoring my jab, she continues by informing me that she is president of the local chapter of PRESERVATIONISTS UNLIMITED.

MS. DIAMONDS AND THE OUTDOOR WRITER

"And, everyone, simply EVERYONE, knows how we condemn such immoral deeds committed by people such as you."

"Well, I'm sorry to say I am not familiar with your "PU", but I am, however, a 32 year sponsor member of DU, and we..."

Without giving me a chance to finish, she declares this disgusting conversation has already given her a headache, and she begs to be excused so she may retire to the powder room to take an "AHspirin".

Her departure leaves me also in need of medication, which my bartender friend quickly administers.

During my reprieve, I remember having heard of "Ms. Diamonds". It seems she has quite a reputation, part of which from her uninhibited college years, would best remain forgotten. However, she has since been widowed three times, with each marriage elevating her social and financial status considerably.

Somewhere along the way her potatoes suddenly became "potAHtoes", and today, she acquired the notoriety of being an extremely outspoken activist in a variety of anti-groups.

While Ms. Diamonds is visiting the powder room, the announcement is made: "Dinner is served."

I breathe a sigh of relief, thinking I'll be saved from having to listen to all of her bombastic rhetoric. But, it is not to be. The prearranged seating at the dinner table places us next to each other shattering my hopes of a pleasant evening. With a pleading expression, I make eye contact with my host, Bill, but I find no solace there. His wink and impish smile says it all: "What do ya think of your dinner partner?"

Evidently her "AHspirin tAHblet" must have worked wonders, for when Ms. Diamonds returns, she continues from where she left off as though she had not been away at all. As I politely hold the chair for her to be seated, she lets me have both barrels.

"It makes me physically ill when I think of how you so-called sportsmen actually relish in devouring the flesh of those beautiful "AHnimals". It is an act I consider closely related to outright cannibalism.

While she is expounding on my lack of morals, she is in the process of relishing her entrée of Beef Wellington. That's when she suddenly realizes her latest ranting may have placed her far out on a vulnerable limb, and a quick glance at my eyes tells her I am just before pouncing on it with saw in hand.

Abruptly, she switches the subject to a more timely dissertation on how she favors legislation abolishing all firearms and how it would immediately do away with the immoral practice of hunting and the senseless slaughter of "AHnimals".

At this point, I am able to slip in a comment on how millions of tax dollars from the sale of arms, ammunition and fishing tackle are annually channeled into conservation projects. But, I'm ignored again, and her endless rhetoric never ceases.

As we continue with dinner, I find, if my timing is right between bites, I can sneak in a word or two. So, I mention how dwindling habitat is a far greater detriment to wildlife than firearms and how the harvest of game, under controlled conditions, is an important tool in the science of wildlife management.

I'm wasting my breath, however, for my views fall on deaf ears. Somewhere in the midst of all her unrelenting sermons, my brain becomes clouded, so in a trance, I tune her out, homing in on thoughts of my own.

Why, I wonder, am I sitting here listening to all of this horse-hockey? Nothing I say is going to influence her in any way whatsoever, and she sure as hell isn't going to change my ways of thinking. I like to fish and hunt, and I enjoy the companionship of some mighty fine people who think as I do.

I revel in feeling a trout at the end of my line before I net and release it, but at the same time, I can savor the delicate flavor of a walleye on my dinner plate without a guilty conscious. To me, there is nothing more thrilling than watching the "ballet-like" movements of a flight of ducks coming into range over my decoys, but it doesn't bother me to dine on char-broiled mallard breasts sautéed in wine sauce and ladled over wild rice.

The rewards I receive from fishing and hunting far exceed those of full creels and game-bags. Simply being outdoors in the environs where wild things dwell, and to become one with the wonders and beauty of nature, is often satisfaction enough.

Who can find fault with cherished moments such as those?

I carry rod and gun afield because it is a part of the challenging quest, but if I should return with nothing; my day has still been a success.

Admittedly, there are individuals who find no interest in such things. That is their prerogative, and they should not be chastised for having their opinions. But, neither should I be for having mine.

My problem with people like Ms. Diamonds is: What gives those pompous-ass screaming hypocrites, the right to claim a higher place in heaven for themselves and a lower place in hell for those of us who love to fish and hunt?

Before answering my own question, I suddenly remember my cardiologist warning me that stress brought on by such pointless and self-argued debates is not good for an erratic ticker, so I fall back and regrouped.

Besides, at my age, time is much too precious to waste debating morals and ethics with all the "Ms. Diamonds" in the world. Hunting and fishing are things I enjoy doing, and they are done at places close in kinship with that heaven I may never reach.

Eventually, our evening as Bill and Penny's guests comes to an end, and as we are thanking them and saying our good-bye's, I experience one last encounter with Ms. Diamonds.

"It has been sooo nice," she says, offering me her limp hand, palm down and gems up.

Wondering if she's expecting me to kiss it, I let it rest in mine and simply mutter, "Likewise."

"And, it has been AHbsolutely delightful meeting you, too, my dear," Ms. Diamonds croons, turning to Pet, "and I must say you do have the most chAHming husband."

I suffer a sudden choking convulsion brought on by an unobserved jab in the ribs from friend Bill's elbow.

SUPPORT
DUCKS UNLIMITED

A VOICE FROM THE PAST
(A War Story Continued)

Part One:
Bougainville Island, Solomon Islands,
November, 1943

During World War II, I was a radio
man with a forward observation team of
the 12th Marine Artillery Regiment.
When we landed on the Japanese held
island of Bougainville, in the Solomon
Islands, we were in trouble from the
start. Contact with the enemy was
always imminent. The place was nothing
but a stinking quagmire of decayed
vegetation in a massive jungle swamp so
dense our vision was limited to but a
few yards at the very most. This
greatly hampered our ability to spot
enemy targets.

229

A VOICE FROM THE PAST

So, our only alternative was to use observation from the air. However, the "SeaBees" had not finished constructing our landing strip, so for the time being our only air cover had to come from Munda on New Georgia Island some 300 miles to the southeast.

We solved this problem by sending one observer from each of our four battalions back to Munda. From there, Navy pilots would fly one of them at a time over Bougainville to spot targets for us from the air.

The plane's fuel capacity allowed them to stay over our front lines about an hour and a half until being relieved by the second spotter, followed by the third and then the fourth. That way we had an observer over us constantly each day, when the weather permitted.

My job was to keep in radio contact with the observer in the plane overhead, receiving the spotter's map coordinates, locating enemy troop concentrations and supply dumps. Then they would advise us of the range and deflection corrections of our artillery rounds falling in the impact area.

My radio code name was "Decoy", and the call signs for our air observers were, "Airspot One", "... Two", "... Three and "... Four". Of our four spotters, "Airspot One" was the best. Somehow, he seemed to have a natural talent for finding enemy positions the others overlooked.

A VOICE FROM THE PAST

A typical air to ground conversation would go something like this:

"HELLO, DECOY... THIS IS AIRSPOT ONE... HOW DO YOU READ ME??? OVER..."

"AIRSPOT ONE... THIS IS DECOY... READING YOU LOUD AND CLEAR... DO YOU HAVE A TARGET FOR US? OVER..."

"DECOY, THIS IS AIRSPOT ONE... FIRE MISSION... FROM CHECK POINT TWO FIVE NINE... DOWN TWO HUNDRED... LEFT ONE HUNDRED... GIVE ME ONE ROUND OF SMOKE TO OBSERVE..."

"ROGER, AIRSPOT ONE... STAND BY..."

One of my buddies, in telephone contact with the firing batteries, would relay the coordinates to the Fire Direction Center of our First Battalion.

"AIRSPOT ONE THIS IS DECOY... ONE ROUND OF SMOKE ON THE WAY..."

Within seconds, the observer would see a column of white smoke rising from the exploding round.

"THIS IS AIRSPOT ONE... DOWN FIVE ZERO... DEFLECTION CORRECT... ONE ROUND H.E. (high explosive) "TO OBSERVE".

"ROGER... STAND BY... ON THE WAY...

"RANGE CORRECT... DEFLECTION CORRECT... FIRE FOR EFFECT..."

"ROGER... STAND BY... FIRING ABLE BATTERY... THREE ROUNDS H.E. (high explosive) FOR EFFECT... ON THE WAY..."

"YOU GOT 'EM, DECOY... CEASE FIRE... MISSION ACCOMPLISHED..."

A VOICE FROM THE PAST

"ROGER, AIRSPOT ONE... THANK YOU... AND OUT..."

Although I had never met that Marine, we talked to each other about every day the weather was clear for flying during the battle for Bougainville. All I knew of him was his rank and last name, Sergeant Connelly, and his radio call sign was "Airspot One".

Since Connelly was so efficient in spotting for us at Bougainville, he was given the airspot job permanently together with a field commission of Second Lieutenant. Consequently, he spotted for us throughout the Guam campaign in July of 1944, and again, in February of 1945 in those hectic days during the battle for Iwo Jima.

Then, while over enemy territory in advance of our front lines, we saw tracers of anti-aircraft fire rising from the ground to strike Airspot One's plane. Trailing smoke, the pilot banked it away to crash land in the sea near one of our ships. We heard later that Connelly had been killed.

Part Two:
Terre Haute, Indiana
May 1995

Earlier in the year, I included the above scenario in a book I had written. It was entitled, "The Last Banzai", and was about my buddies in the 12th Marines during World War II.

A VOICE FROM THE PAST

Shortly after it was published, I began receiving mail orders for it from all over the country. One of those orders was from a man in Texas named Merrill Connelly, and in his letter, he mentioned that he, too, had been in the 12th Marines and had, for a while, worked as a forward observer.

I didn't remember him being one of our front line observers, but when I mailed the copy of my book to him, I included a note calling his attention to those pages that told about the Marine of the same name I had seen shot down and killed at Iwo Jima. I thought perhaps they may have been related or at least, have known each other.

One morning about a week later, while Pet and I were having our morning coffee, the phone rang. When I answered it, a voice said, "Jack Kerins... This is Airspot One."

I couldn't believe it! Nearly fifty years after I had seen him shot down and reportedly killed, I was actually speaking to the same man I had been in radio contact with so many times during the war.

His name was Merrill Connelly, and he told me the pilot had been killed, and he had been injured but was rescued. Needless to say, our telephone reunion was a lengthy, but joyful one, as we reminisced about those unforgettable days.

During our conversation, Merrill asked several questions about writing and publishing a book.

"I've been thinking about doing one myself," he said. "Not about my wartime adventures, but about my brother.

"He was a Navy officer, and we did get to see each other once during the war, when our ship stopped at Kwajalein Atoll when we were on the way to Guam.

"He has had an adventurous life and I believe his life story would make an interesting book.

You see, after his war years, he became Secretary of the Navy under Lyndon Johnson and later he was Governor of Texas. He was also with President Kennedy when he was assassinated in Dallas."

UGLY AND STUPID AT THE SAME TIME

The whole fiasco began shortly after World War II, long before my friend, the Judge, graduated from law school, and we were a couple of young idiots finishing up our college degrees at Indiana State on the G.I. Bill.

It just so happened, the end of the Spring term tied in perfectly with the Memorial Day weekend, giving us a few extra days for a much needed break. One of The Judge's buddies from his Navy fighter squadron, had invited the two of us down to fish a lake on his cotton plantation near Greenville, Mississippi.

It also just so happened we had a local friend who was one of the owners of a flying school at Hulman Field, and who, in one of his weaker moments, following a party at BJ's Rod & Gun Club, very graciously offered to let us

235

use one of his company's air planes to save us travel time going and coming.

Earlier that same spring, a tornado had skipped through the Terre Haute area, and the somewhat antiquated plane we were being loaned was one that had been flipped over in the storm. However, it had been recently fitted with a new wing so, barring complications, our vacation plans seemed to be in good shape.

The day of our departure was bright and sunny with not a cloud in the sky. So by all expectations, we should have had a smooth flight and maybe even get in a little fishing with our host before dinner that evening.

Now, it must be remembered that The Judge had been flying nothing smaller than Navy Corsair Fighters since he had earned his wings in those light training planes at Pensacola.

As for me, I had been a foxhole Marine, whose one and only flying experience was a twenty minute hop I hitched in a B-24 over Guadalcanal.

Anyway, after loading our gear in a small compartment behind the seats, The Judge taxied out to the runway. After letting the engine warm up a minute or two, he began poring the coal to it. Everything was looking good until we began to lift off. That's when, as the saying goes, "The old stuff hit the fan."

Evidently the installation job of that new wing left something to be desired. One side seemed a little out of plumb with the other. The starboard wing began flying a tad early, dropping its counterpart on the port side enough to clip the runway spinning us around and tearing a hole in the cloth fabric.

The Judge, immediately cut the ignition, uttering a disgusted, "DAMN!", and I crossed myself.

Some of the people back at the control tower must have taken the incident with a greater surge of adrenalin than we did. For, even as we were getting our feet on the ground, three emergency vehicles were speeding toward us with sirens blaring and red lights flashing.

The damage assessment proved to be minor, so they gave us a ride as they towed the wounded bird back to the hanger. There they covered the small hole with a fabric patch. So, while waiting for the heat lamps to dry the adhesive dope, The Judge and I had a cup of coffee at the airport restaurant.

Eventually, they announced that repairs had been completed and all was now in good shape. Again, we taxied out to look down the long runway, and His Honor let the engine warm up once more.

All the while, I was mentally questioning my fishing buddy's skills as a pilot and my own sanity for sitting out here beside him ready to give it another go.

"We'll make it this time," pledged The Judge, standing heavily on the brakes and revving the engine until I thought the whole rig would shake apart. But once he released the brake, we rolled only a short distance before popping up in the air. We were on our way at last.

Because of our delay in taking off, the daylight was beginning to fade as we approached Paducah, Kentucky, so we landed at the local airfield, hitched a ride into town, and checked in at the Irving S. Cobb Hotel.

"I'll leave an early wake-up call so we can get out of here shortly after daylight," ruled The Judge.

"Whoa! Hold it just a tad," I objected. "Just so happens I noticed there's a 6 a.m. Mass scheduled at that Catholic Church across the street from this hotel.

"So, if you don't mind, Ol' Buddy, I think I'll slip over there and make myself right with the Lord before I climb back in that hunk of junk with you."

During breakfast, His Honor gave me a quick course in aeronautical navigation. Since we would be heading south, I was to turn the map upside-down, and match the landmarks on the map with those below us.

It all worked perfectly. I picked out Reelfoot Lake in Tennessee, and we were right on course as we flew over Dyersburg, which was at the bottom of my map.

"O.K. Now get the next chart and we'll plot right into Greenville," said my instructor.

That sounded simple enough, but it brought up the first problem of our morning. There was no "next chart".

"Jack, I'm sure I put it in the plane before we left."

"I can't find it," I said, "maybe it got tossed out when they were patching the wing yesterday."

"Oh well, that's O.K. We really don't need it anyway. That's the Yazoo River down there. We'll just follow it into Greenville," he assured me.

This, too, sounded simple enough. But, a short while later, the second problem of our day raised its ugly head.

The spring flood waters we had experienced up north in Indiana a few weeks earlier were now at their peak in Mississippi. Below us the Yazoo River became a part of "The Mighty Miss." and it looked as if we were over an ocean rather than a meandering stream. It spread out of sight in all directions, covering all possible landmarks.

About then, I noticed my trusted pilot was beginning to show signs of concern, checking the compass, his watch, the gas gauge and fiddling with his dead-reckoning computer.

"Damn! We ought to be there, or at least getting close. We're low on gas," he said, banging on the fuel gauge to make sure it wasn't stuck. We had already switched over to the auxiliary tank about an hour before.

Now, we began flying in a huge circle trying to find some kind of an identifying mark to give us a bearing. Finally, on the distant horizon, we spotted a water tower, and we headed for it. "DREW, MISS." Read the lettering painted on its side.

"I remember, Drew from the time I was down here visiting Bobby once before," my pilot said. "Trouble is, I can't remember if it was north, south, east or west of Greenville. But it doesn't make any difference, we're almost out of gas, and we've got to set 'er down... someplace."

Now, he began looking for a strip of pasture land and at last, found something that looked promising. He flew low over the field a couple of times, looking down studying its length and how smooth it appeared to be.

All the while, he was lecturing me on how he was checking to make sure the pasture grass was an even shade of green, and how if there were low spots, like ruts and holes, the grass would be darker because moisture would collect there.

This bit of information did hint that maybe he knew what he's doing after all, but it didn't do much to ease my tension, so I filed it in my memory bank along with other trivia.

"Well, it seems O.K." he said, taking a deep breath. "And we don't have much of a choice, so hang on."

240

UGLY AND STUPID AT THE SAME TIME

We began our approach low and slow, dropping in just past the trees at one end of the field and cutting the ignition, while letting the plane settle in on its own. The landing was surprisingly smooth, and both of us blew a sigh of relief.

When we rolled to a stop, we still had about twenty yards to spare. Unlatching our seat belts, we climbed out, more than happy to have our feet on the ground again.

The fence directly in front of us left no doubt as to where we were. The lettering across its high arched gateway, clearly spelled it out: **MISSISSIPPI STATE PENITENTIARY – Drew, Miss**.

My pilot's only comment was, "WOW!", and I just stood there with my mouth gaping open in disbelief.

We looked around to survey our situation. Beside the fence, not far from us, stood a man wearing a black and white striped shirt and trousers and a wide-eyed expression on his face. He had been hoeing weeds along the fence line and was definitely frightened, doffing his hat and nodding as we approached.

"Is there a telephone somewhere around here?" asked The Judge.

"Oh Yes, Sir... Yes, Sir... That's the warden's house right over there past the gate. He's got a telephone."

We caught the warden and his family just sitting down to dinner.

After introducing ourselves and explaining our problem, he showed us to the wall mounted phone and called the operator for us.

"Hi, Bobby. This is your old squadron buddy," he said, holding the receiver so we could both hear.

"Hey! Where in the hell ya'll been? I was out to the airfield three times lookin' for ya."

"Well, it's kind of a long story," said The Judge. "You see, we kind of ran out of map an' out of gas about the same time, and had to set 'er down. We're over here in the State Penitentiary at Drew."

There was a long pause. Then the soft voice, in its slow and definitely southern accent, came back with, "How's come ya'll is so damned ugly and stupid at the same time?"

Bobby, promised to phone a crop duster friend of his to bring us a can of gas. When we hung up, the warden was interested in hearing all about our little adventure, and invited us to join him at dinner with his family.

When our gas arrived, we thanked the warden, and the whole family stood waving good-bye as we took off for Greenville which was only about forty miles to the southeast.

All things being considered, our little Memorial Day weekend turned out to be a success after all. We had a nice visit with Bobby and his wife, caught a passel of Mississippi brim and

242

even got in a round of golf before flying home.

This was just the first of the many unforgettable adventures The Judge and I have had together over the years. Looking back on it all, in our advanced years, we've had quite an eventful life. But today, we've slowed down quite a bit, and we are beginning to agree with Bobby. We are now both "old and ugly", and to higher degree, "kind of stupid too"... all at the same time.

WAR AND PEACE AND A DOG
NAMED GYPSY

Martin Rodenski's eyes continued to search the gray November sky as the early morning chill began to find its way through his camouflaged insulation. Now and then, as he felt that same old pain in his left shoulder, a low moan escaped his lips.

Beside him in the duck blind, a golden retriever quivered as she snuggled up against his hip boot.

"Guess we're both getting' too old for this game, Gypsy girl," he muttered, rubbing the dog's wet pelt. "That last drake you brought in was almost too much for you, wasn't it?

"Maybe we should start headin' back anyway. It's getting' colder, and it's a long hike to the truck.

WAR AND PEACE AND A DOG NAMED GYPSY

Besides, those clouds rollin' in from the north are lookin' downright mean."

Two days later and some seven hundred miles to the south, Riley McKay was staring at his word processor's blank screen. It was simply one of those times when coming up with a catchy lead for his new magazine article was completely eluding him. He was pressed for time trying to make his deadline, but as he was beginning to picture it all in his mine, the phone rang.

His gruff "HELLO" left no doubt the caller was interrupting something important.

"Riley... Ike McHannon here. Hate to bother you, but I thought you would want to hear about Ski."

"You know my time's always open to you, Ike. What kind of trouble has that big lug gotten himself into this time?"

"He's gone, Riley," said Ike, his voice choking, 'gone to guard the streets.'* The funeral's day after tomorrow. I'm driving up late this evening."

* A quote from the Marine Hymn: "If the Army and the Navy ever look on heaven's scene they will find the streets are guarded by a United States Marine."

WAR AND PEACE AND A DOG NAMED GYPSY

"I'll leave first thing in the morning," said Riley, his voice now soft and sadly concerned. "Book me in with you at the same motel where we stayed before. What happened to him?"

"Evidently he was caught out in a severe blizzard while he was duck hunting. A conservation officer found him about three miles from his pick-up. They think he became disoriented on his way out of the swamp. He and Gypsy are both dead.

"It seems Ski was trying to carry the dog, his old Parker shotgun and a couple mallard drakes when the brunt of the storm overtook them. The stupid idiot had even taken off his coat and wrapped it around Gypsy. That's the way they found them."

Early next morning Riley's odometer was rolling up the miles a little faster than the Wisconsin speed limit allowed. And as he was heading up the northbound lane of US 53 his thoughts were of other times and other places.

It was in the early days of World War II when he first met Ike and Ski. From that day on, their admiration for each other could not have bound them closer if they had been a trio of blood brothers. Together, they shared the best of times along with the worst, even in life and death situations.

Their recruit training and specialized schooling had taken place at the San Diego Marine Corps Base in California. That was followed by two urgent months of advanced military tactics and combat maneuvers before they shipped out to New Zealand.

Next, came the real thing, during those hectic days when our country's future dangled in the balance. The war took them to places they had never heard of before – Guadalcanal and Bougainville in the Solomon Islands. They went there as boys, and came away hardened combat veterans, old before their time.

Following a short rest, they found themselves aboard another transport, this time on the way to the Marianas. As they lay sunning themselves on a hatch cover, they wondered if the war would ever end and if they would ever see their homeland and loved ones again.

"They'll surely relieve us after this one," said Riley.

"They'd better," threatened Ike, "and I mean soon. I'm just before askin' the Lord if I can borrow those special shoes of his so I can take off walkin' home across this damned ocean."

"Yeah!" said Ski. "My folks have a good farm back in Wisconsin, and I've got the most beautiful little, blue eyed, blonde gal just waitin' for Ol' Ski to come home. And when I do, we're getting' married IMMEDIATELY... or maybe even sooner."

However, their hopes were not to be. While the campaign to liberate the island of Guam from the Japanese was still being fought, another was being planned, and before they realized it, they were gasping for breath as they burrowed in the black, volcanic ash of a hellish place called Iwo Jima.

Less than twenty yards in front of them, two machine guns were firing from a camouflaged bunker. Everyone on their section of the beachhead was pinned down, and casualties were mounting.

"WELL, HELL..." yelled Ski, "SOMEONE'S GOT TO DO IT... LET'S GO!"

Knowing exactly what had to be done, the three sprang forward. Keeping low and zig-zagging as they ran. Riley sprinted up the left flank and Ike up the right, drawing fire in their directions and away from Ski. With a primed grenade in each hand, that big Marine dashed up the center, straight for the bunker.

Then, everything happened at once. Riley dove into the sand when he felt a burning sensation in his left calf, as a bullet tore through his canvas legging, and Ike went down when he was struck in both thighs.

Ski made it all the way to the bunker and shoved his grenades in the two open gun ports. But, he never heard the muffled blasts from inside. They were lost in the deafening roar of a heavy mortar shell exploding a few yards behind him.

Ike and Ski were both evacuated to a hospital ship off shore and later to a Naval hospital at Pearl Harbor. Riley survived, with just a minor wound, to continue fighting the battle for Iwo Jima. His greatest pain came from not knowing if his best buddies were alive or dead, and he was not to find out until six months later when he was rotated back to the United States.

The very day he arrived at the San Diego Marine Corps Base a tearful, but joyful, reunion took place. Ike had just that day been released from Balboa Hospital where Ski was still recouping from his more serious wounds.

"They didn't think he was going to make it for a long time," said Ike. "The doctor on the hospital ship actually saved him when he removed the whole tail-fin section of that mortar round from the back of his left shoulder. The damned thing weighed more than thirteen ounces and had twisted in under his collar bone. It took them almost two hours to get it out."

"How's he doing now?" asked Riley.

"Well, a bad infection set in at first, but he licked that. Now, that hole in his back is beginning to heal. But, there's something else, Riley, and there's not much can be done.

"You see, his folks were notified he was in the hospital here in San Diego, and they were on their way out here to see him when they were both killed in a highway accident. Then, to top it all off, that 'beautiful, blue-eyed blonde gal' of his ran off and married some guy Ski had never heard of.

WAR AND PEACE AND A DOG NAMED GYPSY

"Now, he doesn't give a damn if he lives or dies."

In the years that followed, Riley and Ike both made it a point to check on Ski now and then, but he became more and more despondent, refusing to associate with anyone and finding little, if anything, that held his interest. He sold the farm in Wisconsin and built a lakeside cabin in a remotely wooded area of Minnesota.

The proceeds from the family homestead and his monthly disability check from the Veterans Administration were more than enough to take care of him for the rest of his life, but he was always getting into a variety of troubles – some quite serious.

He began hitting the booze, heavily at times, and even though the pain in his shoulder limited full strength in his left arm, the big guy was constantly getting involved in some barroom brawl that usually resulted in personal injury to his adversary and property damage to the establishment.

After several rescue missions to bail him out, Riley and Ike soon found themselves on a first name basis with the sheriff of Ski's county. However, following each incident, it seemed a period of peace returned – for a short time at least.

Just being with his old wartime buddies again on these short occasions definitely had a positive affect on Ski. Riley and Ike eventually came to recognize this, and while such repeated

251

calls for help disrupted their own lives, those short reunions with Ski meant a great deal to them as well.

"I think his future collapsed when that gal left him," said Ike. "He never got over it. Now, he's just plain lonesome."

"You may be right," agreed Riley. "Maybe we should try getting together with him more often - you know, doing something or going somewhere together, maybe scheduling it at different times. That way he would have something to look forward to. It might be just what he needs. In fact, it could work out best for all three of us."

Their trial run for Ski's rehab program was carried out with some skepticism, but Riley's prediction could not have been more on the mark.

That first summer called for a fishing trip to a fly-in lake in the Canadian bush country where they were on their own, just the three of them, roughing it together in the "boondocks" again. It was kind of like old times, and it was more successful than they could have believed possible.

Later that fall, a pheasant hunt together in South Dakota went over so great that an elk hunt in Montana and a trek to Wyoming for antelope was suggested for the same time frame in the coming year.

In between, a couple of weekend fishing jaunts and duck hunts, right there in Ski's backyard, were added as fillers. But, perhaps the best idea they had was a couple of days together during the Christmas holidays.

Riley hosted the first one at his home, where his family and Ike's adopted Ski as one of their own. It was wonderful, and when the decision was made to rotate the event each year, Ski insisted on it being at his place next time.

That was the Christmas when Riley's gift to Ski was a golden retriever pup. It was a small female, in fact the runt of the litter, but she was well bred and came from a kennel in Iowa operated by a trainer who was a personal friend of Riley's.

Ski named the dog "Gypsy", and for the next fifteen years, the two were inseparable. She completely turned his life around. And, as it happened, the two were together even to the end.

When Riley arrived at the motel, Ike handed him a copy of the local newspaper. The front page article read:

"LOCAL AREA MAN PERISHES IN STORM"

"J. Martin Rodenski was found today, partially buried in the heavy snow from Tuesday's blizzard. The body was discovered several miles from his car by Conservation Officer, Rob Schmidt, who had become acquainted with Rodenski when the two worked together on several area environmental projects. Rodenski was also instrumental in founding the local chapter of Ducks Unlimited, and was awarded the Conservationist-Of-The-Year Award by

the State Department of Natural Resources.

"He was a decorated World War II Marine, and a recipient of the Silver Star and the Purple Heart.

"The body will be laid to rest in a private ceremony on the hillside property owned by Rodenski, and overlooking Lake Wabasheni. Full military rites will be conducted at the grave site by a detachment of Marines led by Lt. Col. Wayne Hendrex, USMC. Two of Rodenski's close comrades from his service days in the Marine Corps will assist."

No mention was made of the fact that Ski and Gypsy were buried together in the same grave, but it was not overlooked by Riley and Ike.

About a month later, the two returned for one last time to oversee the placement of the granite marker they had ordered. The inscription was simple:

J. MARTIN RODENSKI

AUGUST 12, 1922 – NOVEMBER 29, 2003

AND

"GYPSY"

DECEMBER 1987 – NOVEMBER 29, 2003

SEMPER FIDELIS

BEYOND THE PORTAGE

"It's good to be back again," he thought, "mighty good."

A coronary and slow recovery had delayed his return for several years, but the area of the "Little River", as he called it, was pretty much as he remembered it to be.

Among the untold number of streams in the vast Canadian bush country, this comparatively small and nameless flowage seemed insignificant. Nevertheless, it was an important part of the ecosystem. It still ran clear and cold even though it had known the presence of man.

His illness and advancing age had slowed him considerably, and it had taken a lengthy discussion to convince his doctor the trip was exactly what he needed. For this is a quiet and time in the world to breathe in a crisp freshness he had found in but few other places.

The pressure of daily schedules and cluttered calendars were behind him now. Here, his most important cares involved such things as watching an eagle soaring high overhead, or a doe and fawn browsing on watercress in a shallow bay, or perhaps, a beaver gnawing on the trunk of a young birch.

The dip of his paddle and the muted lap of water against the bow were the only sounds as his canoe moved slowly upstream against the gentle current.

Ahead, a bend in the river formed a horseshoe passing high bluffs of ancient granite. He rested his paddle across the gunwales to observe the crystalline quartz and flakes of mica glistening in the morning sun.

This was an outcropping of the Precambrian Shield. Hidden deep within its ageless mantle rest the mysteries of the earth's creation and the rich mineral deposits that often gave reason for maddening quests to satisfy the greed of man.

Around the bend, he paddled past a burn on the west bank. It had come to be years ago when lightning struck in the forest. He remembered helping the wardens fight the fire, and they had won. Although, there are some who would advocate letting it burn, because it was started by a natural cause.

BEYOND THE PORTAGE

Perhaps their theory has some merit, he thought, but he and the wardens were there at the time, as was the lightning, and stopping the consuming blaze seemed to be the right thing for them to do. And, they found satisfaction in preserving the wilderness, for the tomorrows cannot afford its loss.

Green plants and thin saplings were now topping out above the charred stumps and blackened earth, and he marveled at how quickly the wounded land was healing itself.

Farther on, the river spread out in a wide, lake-like basin. At its north end, a rapid roared in from a source hidden higher up in the dense forest, but the raging white water eventually quelled where it came to exit into the basin.

Nearby, he beached his canoe, and sat to rest and watch the eddies swirl out into the more placid river. He was feeling better than he had for a long time, but he remembered promising the doctor he would take it easy and relax now and then.

But, the urge to move on shortened his break, and with backpack riding high on stooped shoulders, he lifted the lightweight craft overhead to begin his carry up the steep bypass skirting the rapid. The trail was old and worn but new grasses and tiny seedlings were creeping in from both sides as they continued their attempt at a natural reclamation.

BEYOND THE PORTAGE

One can learn much from crossing a portage. Along the way, he sees where a bear has rooted out the decaying stump of a fallen balsam, probably grubbing for ants.

Pausing to ponder the site, he concluded that of all the creatures in the forest, this shaggy, black critter could claim the undisputed right to be here. Not just because of his might, but because of what he represents.

There must always be a place for the bear to wander, for without him, there will be forever lost the basic truth of what wilderness is all about.

Plodding along up the incline, he finds that a strong windstorm has downed several trees along the east side of the portage. It created a small clearing now exposed to the sunlight. Here, he rested his canoe beside the trail, and while gathering tiny, but sweet, wild strawberries, he came across the remains of a wolf kill from last winter.

Patches of deer hair and broken bones are scattered about. It is a sad scene. But, here in the wild, death can often be harsh and sudden, and the tragic and violent passing of one species has meant survival for another.

Looking upon the spectacle causes him to evaluate his own role as a hunter and fisherman. He takes from the forests and waters what he needs for his table, and in doing so he depletes the resources by just that much. Yet, he finds comfort in his rationalization that it all seems to fit into the cycle, and the balance, and scheme of things in the ecosystem.

This, he feels, is acceptable as long as his harvest is kept within the ethical bounds of his needs and not credited to the piracy of his greed. For like the wolf, man is a predator, and like the wolf, he is here.

In the end, it is only man who feels the compulsion to explain and account for his behavior here. For that matter, it is only he who needs to.

The trail pitches downhill now, and a little farther on, it exits from the forest at the edge of Snowshoe Lake. Nearby, its deep blue waters spill over into the long, narrow gorge to form the rapids he has just traversed. It is the source of the stream he has named the "Little River".

A huge, slab of granite slopes into the water of the lake, and its surface is streaked with inlays of white and rose quartz. This would make a beautiful campsite, but his day is yet young, so he sits to rest and study his map before floating his canoe once again.

Snowshoe Lake is more than four miles wide and twice as long. He had fished here years ago when he first came with his father. They never reached the far end of the lake or crossed the next portage, but the challenge still remained. So, following his rest, he slid his canoe into the water once more.

"This will be a long paddle", he murmured to himself, "but I'm feeling good, and I may never have the opportunity again."

By the time he had paddled the full extent of Snowshoe and found where the portage leading to the upper chain of lakes, it was late in the afternoon. The wind had been in his favor this day, but now he was feeling the tiredness of his long stint at bending into the paddle. Besides, he thought, this would be a good place to camp before making that rough two mile carry in the morning.

The same lake he had just crossed rewarded him with a succulent dinner of walleye fillets. Now, he sat beside his stone-ringed fire, and as he sipped his coffee, he remembered another canoe trip he had taken just prior to his hear attack.

His companion had been a trapper who spent most of his life in the Canadian bush. Old "Moose" has since passed away, he remembered, but his gruff voiced sentiments bore the same element of truth today as they did that night eight years ago.

"Damned if I know how any son-of-a-bitch can have an evil thought when he's lookin' in a fire."

Crude? Yes, but he still liked the connotation. It cut away the rhetoric and got down to the basics. Every camp fire he had known has been like that. They have a way of humbling a man, putting him in his place, you might say.

His canoe had served him well this day. Now, it rested a few feet back from his fire, propped up on one side by a couple of Y-shaped branches. With his sleeping bag spread beneath, it made a comfortable lean-to and reflected the heat from the glowing embers in front of it. He had never ventured into the bush country without a canoe.

The coming of the floatplane had made easy access to these vast, trackless areas once known only to the Ojibwa, the Cree and a few trappers. Now, the wilderness was open to an ever increasing number of modern day adventurers. But flying is a hurried and impersonal way to explore. It is only by paddling and on foot that one can really come to know the wilderness.

A canoe is more than just a means of transportation, he thought. In this lonesome land of rivers, lakes and forests, it is like an old friend – one a man can occasionally speak to and shares his thoughts with.

He can feel it respond to his paddle, and it becomes a part of him, and he of it. With a personality all its own, it is not unlike a vulnerable young lady, he decided. For it is a fragile thing, demanding love and special care. And, like the lady, it has feelings, moods, and at times, surprises he must learn to live with.

BEYOND THE PORTAGE

In return for the faith and trust he places in it, his canoe will fulfill his need for survival in this wilderness he has come to know and love.

On this evening, as he sat sipping his coffee, his fire was burning low. So, with the tow of his boot, he shoved a piece of wood deeper into the coals, producing a shower of sparks and new life to the glowing embers.

Again, he fell victim to the enchantment of watching the small blazes flare up and subside. His worldly cares drifted away with the rising smoke. Only time itself was of major importance to him.

After all, he remembered some philosopher once saying, "Time is the measuring stick of history – a time that was, a time that is, and a time that is yet to come."

Shaking his head, he broke the spell of a mind drifting in trivia. By now, he was feeling extremely tired from the effects of his long and strenuous day.

He poured the remaining coffee on the dying embers and crawled into his sleeping bag beneath the canoe. He drifted off quickly, and in his final thoughts, he wondered about tomorrow and what awaited him.

As the sun rose in a cloudless sky the next morning, all was quiet and serene at the little campsite. By now, the ashes in the fire ring were cold, and the only sounds were the soft breeze rustling through the pines and the mournful wailing of a loon echoing across a lake somewhere beyond the long portage.

* * *

This story first appeared in "SPORTING TALES MAGAZINE"

DYING EMBERS

"Be a good boy, mind you Ma and Pa, an' be kind to birds, an' dogs an' old folks."

He was satisfied he had chosen the appropriate words to end a visit with his young grandson. After all, he could see nothing wrong with advising respect for parental authority. And, being humane with critters, both wild and tame, can be rewarding in many ways.

As for showing a bit of compassion for old codgers, well... Maybe he was just feeling kinda sorry for himself – "involutional melancholia" – or whatever it is the psych boys call it. He rationalized it as being just another prerogative allowed someone his age.

It fit right well with other privileges granted a graybeard, such as being sot in his ways and expounding a lot on his past, kinda like taking inventory of his assets now and then.

"Adventures?" He'd had a passel of them. Far more than the average man, he figured.

"Friends?" An even greater and highly valued number than he deserved.

"Successes and failures?" Heavier on the first, and the latter wasn't worth dwelling on anyway.

"Riches?" By monetary standards, about par, but through it all, he had been blessed with the most wonderful, patient, and understanding wife and three of the finest children a man could hope to have.

"Living it over again?" There'd be damned few things he'd change – if any, he thought. The only thing, perhaps, would be a different ending for this book, but what the hell, it got him to where he was going, didn't it?

As an afterthought, he might have added, "I'll see ya in the spring."

ABOUT THE AUTHOR
Jack Kerins

An avid outdoorsman, Jack's life has been one adventure after another. In his words, "It all began when I was a kid growing up on Grandma Jenuine's farm in Vermillion County, Indiana, and it's still going on today... even though I'm now old, ugly and kinda stupid all at the same time."

During World War II, he was a combat Marine participating in the battles of Guadalcanal, Bougainville, Guam and Iwo Jima.

In later years, his free-lance writing and photography has taken him all over the United States and from the steaming jungles of Central America to the vast reaches of the Arctic.

When television was in its infancy, he hosted one of the nation's first outdoor programs. It continued weekly for twenty-one years.

He is a member of the Outdoor Writers Association of America, and a past-president of the Association of Great Lakes Outdoor Writers. Many of his articles and photographs have received excellence-in-craft awards, and in 1978, he was named Outdoor Writer of the Year by the Indiana Department of Natural Resources.

In 2002, he was inducted into the National Freshwater Fishing Hall of Fame as a "Legendary Communicator".